FINDING FOREVER

A Novella Written By: Keisha Ervin

P.O. Box 2535
Florissant, Mo 63033

Edited by: Terra Little
Proof Reader: Lynel Johnson-Washington
Cover Designed by Sheldon Mitchell of Majaluk and Brenda Hampton

Manufactured in the United States of America

Library of Congress Control Number: 2008933631

ISBN 13: 978-0-9816483-4-7
ISBN 10: 0-9816483-4-7

For information regarding discounts for bulk purchases, please contact Prioritybooks Publications at 1-314-306-2972 or rosbeav03@yahoo.com

You can contact the author at: keisha_ervin2002@yahoo.com

FINDING FOREVER

Published by Prioritybooks Publications

DEDICATION

Jay, you came into my life at the perfect time. I prayed for years for someone like you to come along. Who would've thought that the whole time you were right underneath my nose? I've truly been blessed by your presence. You've changed my life in ways I never thought imaginable. My heart's dictionary defines you. If heaven had a height you'd be that tall. With you I feel a deep and tender, inevitable feeling of undeniable oneness.

ACKNOWLEDGEMENTS

Lord, in the past year you have seen and guided me through some of my most trying times. There were moments when I thought I was being punished or I didn't think I could go on, but your strength carried me. Thank you for helping me through the storm. Now I can humbly say that the light is shining through. I pray that I can continue to live my life according to your word and not my own.

Kyrese!!! You've grown so much, my beautiful baby. You're my angel. My heart couldn't love another person on this earth more. Every time I look into those big ole brown eyes of your eyes, I melt. No one loves you more than I do. You've been my sidekick throughout this journey and I wouldn't want anyone else to be by my side. I LOVE YOU, WOODA!!!!!

Mama, thank you so much for standing by my side and helping me when I'm at my lowest. I know that if I can't count on anyone else, I can always count on you. You always have my best interests at heart. I love you.

Daddy and Keon, I love you!!!

To my girls, Locia, Sharissa, Monique, TuShonda and Ashley, words can't describe how much your friendship means to me. I love you all.

Mike, you are truly my brother from another mother. Love you, kid.

Rose, I thank you from the bottom of my heart for this opportunity. This project fell into my lap when I needed it most. Thank you!!!

Brenda Hampton, not only are you my agent and a colleague, but my friend. You have had my back when some didn't. You are a truly blessed and gifted person. I love you and thank you.

Last but certainly not least, are my fans. You all don't know what your words of encouragement do for me. You all are the reason I can continue to write. Thank you all for riding with me these past four years. I pray that we can continue down this journey of discovery together. I love you!!!

Please feel free to contact me at keisha_ervin2002@yahoo.com or www.myspace.com/keishaervin

CHAPTER ONE

Sweet November

It was one of those rare days where everything seemed to be perfect for Koran McKnight. The sun was in full view, shining brightly, emphasizing the pearl colored hue on his Range Rover. Rick Ross' smash hit, "Boss," thumped loudly through the Pioneer speakers, sending shockwaves into the city streets. There wasn't a cloud in sight and the forecast for the day was seventy degrees with no chance of rain.

Koran was invigorated. A blunt filled with the finest weed hung from the corner of his lips. He had a fresh haircut and the fat wad of money that lay folded in his pocket reminded him that struggling was a thing of the past. For years he'd endured hell on the streets, only to finally see heaven. Like most, Koran was searching for forever, that feeling of everlasting bliss and tranquility. But since as far back as he could remember all he knew were long nights under the streetlight.

So in his mind every now and then he deserved the right to floss. With the kind of life he led, it was a miracle he lived to see his seventeenth birthday. Growing up in Wellston, one of the most poverty-stricken sections of St. Louis City, wasn't a fairytale. It was either go hard or go home. If you were soft the streets were sure to take you under. Koran knew that the world was a cold and bitter place, but the block was as hot as a stove.

Niggas banged over sets and colors. Innocent bystanders were robbed and killed. Young women lost their souls and prostituted their bodies for the euphoric sensation of heroin being shot into their veins. Koran could vividly remember the nights when his stomach ached and growled from hunger as he hustled to make dough. He'd witnessed the fiends he sold rock to overdose on the poison that afforded him new jewelry and clothes. He could

1

envision walking in on his mother as she lay on the bathroom floor in a comatose state, with blow up her nose.

The corner was no joke. For years it was his monument to success. It afforded him the finer things in life, but it was also a place where struggle and greed fought on a daily basis for victory. He'd played with the idea of going the square route and attending college, but Koran was a street nigga to the heart. Getting money the illegal way was all he knew and after years of hustling, Koran no longer had to battle the block for supremacy.

He now had a small crew of niggas who worked the corner for him. At the age of twenty-five, Koran had things that most dope boys only dreamed of. At night, he lay comfortably in a three-hundred-thousand dollar crib in the heart of South St. Louis City. He possessed three expensive cars and stayed dipped in the latest fashions.

A red Philly cap rested low, covering his Asian inspired eyes and long locs hung past his shoulders. Three carat diamond stud earrings gleamed from his ears, highlighting his peanut butter colored skin. Chiseled cheekbones, a button nose and soft, kissable lips made up the rest of his facial features. A sleeve of tattoos covered both of his arms, while a huge portrait of a flying eagle decorated the right side of his neck. Koran was that dude and although he was very humble you couldn't tell him he wasn't the shit.

Bobbing his head to the beat, he pulled up to the stoplight slowly. Inhaling smoke from the blunt, Koran took a look over to his right and spotted the finest woman he'd ever been blessed to see. She was everything the corner was not, overwhelmingly beautiful with skin the shade of golden wheat grass. From what Koran could see of her she looked to be voluptuously thick. And, yes, there were circumstances in his life that should've prevented him from pursuing her, but at that moment all he knew was that he had to have her.

"Excuse me, sweetheart," he said as he leaned his left arm out of the driver side window to get her attention.

"Yes," the girl replied, turning down the volume on the radio.

"I don't mean to bother you, but I just had to know what your name and number are, so I could call you sometime."

Never forgetting a face or a voice, the girl removed the shades shielding her eyes and smiled.

"Whitney," she laughed before pulling off.

Caught off guard by her reply, Koran sat dumbfounded. It had been eight years since he'd laid eyes on her, but the name Whitney would forever be embedded in his memory museum. She was the definition of the truth. The time they spent together was equivalent to being able to fly. No other women in life would ever compare. She was his first love and his best friend. She was his encouragement when the world put him down.

She loved him when he wasn't loveable. She consoled him when his mother overdosed on his stash. Whitney gave him money when his pockets were low. But all of that came to an abrupt end on a cold November afternoon when they were seventeen.

They were outside waiting for her bus when she suddenly broke down and cried. Koran pressed for answers as to why tears fell from her eyes, but the words Whitney wanted so desperately to convey would not pour from her mouth. It was as if they were stuck on pause in the center of her throat. Still perplexed as to why she was upset, Koran requested that she give him a call when she got home. Whitney agreed, knowing fully well that after that moment the two would never see each other again.

For months Koran wondered why. He couldn't understand how she could just pick up and leave with no goodbye. To the world, he cursed her name, but deep down inside he was internally sick. How could he love her so much and live with the fact that she was gone? Fate couldn't be that cruel. Or could it? These were things that Koran struggled with as dreams of Whitney's sweet lips engulfed his mind. Everything from the memory of her perfume to the way she wore her hair plagued his soul during those lonely nights under the streetlight.

It took time, but Koran's frozen heart finally unthawed and healed. Now, eight years later, here she was and all the questions he'd stored up could be answered. Eager to catch up with her, Koran pressed his foot on the gas and followed Whitney down Delmar Boulevard and into the Delmar Loop. The Delmar Loop was a six-block area with boutiques, specialty shops, restaurants, galleries and live entertainment. After parking his truck behind her car they both stepped out into the warm spring air.

Koran couldn't deny her sex appeal. Whitney looked even better up close. Her long black hair was set in big wavy curls, accentuating her doe-shaped eyes. Just as he remembered, ocean deep dimples sank each of her cheeks. Whitney's lips were so pouty and pink that he wanted nothing more than to spend hours kissing them.

Koran wasn't the only one to take notice of her beauty. Every man in the vicinity admired her frame. She was a size fourteen and curvy in all the right places. That day she was dressed casually chic. A pair of oversized gold hoop earrings swung from her ears, and on her neck she wore a gold necklace with a leaf pendant. A white racer-back tank top showcased her 36C breasts, while dark denim pencil-leg capris enhanced her thighs and calves. On her feet she rocked a brand new pair of gold BCBG heels.

Activating the alarm on his truck, Koran watched as she moved to open the back door to her car. The way she moved was like something straight out of a music video. Whitney's hips swayed with the wind. After releasing London, her two-year-old rottweiler, she happily made her way toward him.

"Goddamn, I ain't seen you in a minute," Koran stressed as she approached.

"I know. I was just thinkin' about you."

"Really?"

"Yeah, I was wondering if you still wore the same cologne," she replied, taking a whiff of his neck. "You don't, but you still smell good." Whitney smiled nervously. "It's been a long time, Koran."

"Give a nigga a hug then." He spread his arms wide for a hug.

"You know I got you."

"I missed you, girl." Koran inhaled her scent and pulled her close. Whitney smelled just as heavenly as he remembered. "You look good."

"Thanks, so do you."

"Where you been?" he asked, reluctantly letting her go.

"Chicago."

"Word? And you couldn't tell me that eight years ago?" he shot back, unable to hold his feelings back.

"Koran, believe me I wanted to but . . . there was a lot of stuff going on back then that I couldn't talk to you about."

"Like what?"

"Well, for starters, my parents were having problems and on top of that my father's job wanted him to relocate to Chicago. So we moved," she lied.

"What was so hard about that, that you couldn't tell me?"

"What wasn't hard? I didn't want to leave you . . . and I knew it would be hard for me to say goodbye, so I didn't. At the time I thought I was making the best decision for the both of us."

"Yeah, well, you didn't," Koran said with an attitude. "You know how many nights I waited for you?"

"I know. I'm sorry."

"Yeah, you sorry alright."

"Look, I know that saying I'm sorry is like shit to you right now, but you not gon' stand here and talk to me crazy. When I say I'm sorry I mean it. Koran, I swear on everything I love that I never meant to hurt you," Whitney spoke sincerely.

Koran wanted to hate her. His gut ached for the feeling, but the love that took up space in his heart was selfish. His beloved Whitney was back and hopefully here to stay. Nothing could be better. There was no way he was letting her get away twice in one lifetime. The stars in the sky had aligned them together for a reason. And, yes, the feelings he'd once had for her should've been long gone, but the connection they shared was indefinable.

"I feel you, ma. It's all good," Koran replied in a softer tone.

"You sure?" she asked concerned.

"Whitney."

"Okay." She threw up her hands in defeat. "I was just checkin'."

"Where you heading?" Koran changed the subject. He knew Whitney wasn't telling him everything, but he decided to leave the conversation alone for now.

"I was about to take my dog for a walk."

"Can I join you?"

"I guess," she teased. "I'm just playin', c'mon, London." She pulled her dog along.

"Man, what you doing wit a rottweiler? You know you are too little for that big ass dog."

"Maybe I like big things," she said, smirking.

"Look at you, tryin' to talk all nasty," he teased as they walked side by side.

"Boy, whateva. I'm grown now."

"I'm just fuckin' wit you, but tell me how long you been back?"

"About a year."

"Straight, what you been up to?"

"Working and studying for my degree, that's about it."

"That's what's up? What you going to school for?" he asked as they stopped at the end of the street before crossing.

"To be a doctor," Whitney smiled, proud of herself.

"Let me guess, to become a pediatrician."

"How you know?"

"'Cause, I remember you talkin' about it when we were younger."

"Yeah, I love working with kids."

"On the real though, Whitney . . . I can't believe I'm seeing you right now." Koran licked his lips and eyed her hungrily.

"Me either," she replied, slightly anxious.

The entire scene was too good to be true. Above them, the sun was beginning to set, causing a pink tint to cascade over the horizon. A quiet but soft breeze swept over each of their bodies as they stood gazing into each other's eyes. Nothing could be better. Whitney was intoxicated with desire and Koran was her designated driver. For years she'd fantasized about the possibility of being in his presence again, but now that they were face-to-face and the reality of her dreams were coming true, Whitney began to feel suffocated.

"It was good seeing you again, Koran, but it's getting late. I think it's best that I go," she announced before trying to walk away.

"Where you going? Don't walk away from me like that." He grabbed her arm and pulled her back.

"Look, this little reunion was nice, but whatever it is you're after I'm not in the mood for giving. So let's just say goodbye now and part ways as friends."

"You lost your fuckin' mind? Who you think you talkin' to?"

"Koran, I ain't tryin' to argue wit you. All I'm sayin' is—"

"Fuck, what you tryin' to say. What you should be sayin' is my number is . . ." He grabbed her waist and cupped her chin.

"C'mon, Koran, let's just leave the past in the past."

"Fuck the past. Right now I'm lookin' at my future." He glared dead in her eyes.

"Will you stop?" Whitney said, becoming aggravated.

"I'm just gettin' started."

"But I already got a man."

"Stop lying, you ain't seeing nobody."

"Okay, but I'm not lookin' for a relationship."

"Who said anything about a relationship? Slow down, ma, I ain't tryin' to wife you just yet. We could at least have dinner and see a movie first," Koran joked.

"You play too much," she giggled, hitting him in his chest.

"You the one playin'. I'm being dead serious right now."

"You not gon' give up, are you?"

"Nope."

Whitney knew that she should walk away and pretend the last fifteen minutes of her life hadn't happened, but the feeling in the pit of her stomach was too good to let go. She was overcome with anticipation of what could be. Koran had her in the palm of his hand and didn't even know it. A request wasn't even needed. He could have her anyway he wanted.

"I'll give you my number, but only on one condition," she negotiated.

"What's that?" Koran replied as his right thumb caressed the side of her face.

"You have to promise that we'll be strictly friends and that you won't start catching feelings for me again."

"That's a promise I can't keep."

"Why not?"

"'Cause it's already too late."

FINDING FOREVER

Quiet and dark was the setting as Koran unlocked the door and entered the house. It was three o'clock in the morning and even though he should've been tired, Koran felt as if he'd just risen. His run-in with Whitney was the blessing he'd been praying for. Overjoyed, Koran ascended the steps and made his way toward the bedroom. Flashing lights from the television screen danced across the walls.

Unable to go to sleep, Koran kicked off his sneakers, grabbed the remote control and climbed into bed fully clothed. With his hand behind his head, Koran lay flicking through the channels aimlessly. His mind should've been on the kilos of cocaine that were coming in but, instead, pictures of Whitney's golden brown eyes lingered in his mind. Nothing about her had changed and innocence still lie behind her smile.

"Hi, baby," Trina, his ex-girlfriend of four years, said groggily, interrupting his thoughts.

Koran twisted his head to the right, looked at her face and replied, "What's up?" He'd completely forgotten she was there.

"I left you a plate in the microwave."

"Thanks." He turned his attention back to the television, uninterested.

"I missed you."

"That's what's up, but umm . . . I'm gettin' ready to watch TV so ah . . . you can go back to sleep."

"Okay, baby." Trina turned back over and closed her eyes. "I love you."

"Yeah . . . I love you, too."

Finding Forever

Koran rocked back and forth with his hands in his pockets, bored out of his mind. Racks, shelves and tables of overly priced clothes surrounded him. Why Trina had insisted on his accompanying her to buy Malik, her eight-year-old son, summer clothes was beyond him. He could've easily hit her off with a stack and been on his way. They weren't together anymore, but that was a concept Trina didn't seem to understand. Besides, Koran had moves to make. There was pressing business in the streets that he needed to take care of.

Plus, he didn't like being around Trina for too long. At any given moment she was known to pop off with an attitude and spazz out if she didn't get her way. Trina was a drama queen. Under the phrase in the dictionary there should have been a picture of her face. Her fucked up attitude was one of the reasons Koran had left her alone. He couldn't deal with the nonstop arguing and fighting, and what had turned him off even more was that they used to do it in front of her son.

Koran tried to explain to Trina that when a child sees his parents fight it changes him. Koran knew this all too well. For years, he watched his mother and father fight night after night. There was always a constant war going on in their house. His parents, Kora and Sly, were always at each other's throats and they could never agree on anything. One of them had to be right, which would make the other wrong, and that in itself would lead to another argument.

But one day the fighting got to be too much for Sly. He grew tired of the never-ending back and forth, tit for tat nonsense and left. Kora never saw it coming. She thought she and Sly would always be together, despite the fact that they couldn't get along. She didn't think their arguing was that big of a deal, when she did everything possible to ensure that he was happy in every other way.

Kora cooked, cleaned, sucked, fucked and babysat his bullshit for over ten years, so how dare he leave her alone to cope with the fact that he had given up on loving her? Coming to that conclusion was too much for her to deal with, so she didn't. Instead, she coated her pain with denial and alcohol. A couple of glasses of wine lessened the sting and she started having a few glasses a day. Then a girlfriend introduced her to weed. Little did Kora know that her girlfriend's weed was always laced with cocaine. Kora was instantly hooked.

From then on things in her life went downhill. Snorting lines of cocaine quickly took the place of Philly Blunts filled with weed, and soon Kora fell in love with a boy named Heroin. He was the greatest love of them all. Heroin did things to her no other man had ever done. She didn't have to argue with him. He understood her every want and need. Being with him was better than sex. Being in his presence peaked her senses and when he grabbed her arm tightly and pushed himself deep in her veins it was the best euphoric high she'd ever felt.

Heroin took her mind off the thoughts that haunted her and he always came running when she called. He reminded her that with him everything would be okay. He'd become her pimp and like the trick she was, Kora gave all of her money to him. Then, like in every relationship, she and Heroin began to have problems. He started to consume her life in ways she hadn't imagined.

One day Kora woke up to find a man she didn't know on top of her, naked. All of the utilities in her house had been turned off, the furniture had been sold and no food was in the refrigerator. What made her feel even worse was the look of pure disgust in Koran's eyes as he sat in a corner of the room watching her. It was written all over his face that he knew she loved Heroin more than she loved him. Koran was ashamed of her and what she had become. She was no longer his idol. Kora wasn't the beauty she once was. She was a prostitute, a manipulator, a thief, a liar and a junkie, all wrapped up in one.

Kora knew she needed help. She couldn't run away from the pain in her heart forever, so she got back on her feet and dusted her shoulders off. For a minute everything was cool. Kora went to rehab for a month, but Heroin wouldn't leave her alone. They had a bond that was not to be broken. How dare she treat him like their relationship was a casual fling? What they shared was more sacred than a vow or ring. Fuck all the negative things her family and friends had to say. He loved her and he was willing to do anything to get her back.

There wasn't a day that went by where he didn't chase her or call out to her. All he wanted was for her to come see him so they could spend some time together. He knew deep down inside she missed his company, too. At night he watched outside her window as Kora longed for his touch. Tears streamed down her cheeks at the thought of him. The feelings she had for him made her bones ache.

Kora tried to stay away, but eventually she came running back just like Heroin thought she would. But Heroin wasn't going to go easy on her. Kora needed to be taught a lesson. She'd been a very naughty girl. They couldn't go through this again. Kora couldn't take it and neither could Heroin. This time their relationship would be until death do them part. Koran was twelve when his mother overdosed on the only man he'd ever really known, Mr. H.

"What you think about this?" Trina turned around and held up a Polo shirt.

"It's cool. I like it."

"Are you even gon' pick out anything?"

"I mean, Trina, what do you want me to do? I told you I had shit to do today. Any other time you go shopping by yourself. Why you need me to come so bad today?"

"'Cause . . ." she stalled.

"'Cause what?" Koran cocked his neck and gave her a look that said hurry up and think of a lie.

"Malik's getting bigger and I figured you could help me pick him out some big boy clothes. You know how he loves to look like you."

"Yeah, okay, Trina, you just wanted to spend some time wit me." Koran chuckled as he checked his phone.

His boy, Sheek, would be calling soon to give him an update on one of his workers who was being released from jail.

"What you doing later? I'm thinking about making a roast." Trina slowly roamed through the clothes.

"I don't know."

"You should come over and have dinner with me and Malik. He would love to have you there."

"And you wouldn't?" Koran replied sarcastically.

"Did I say that? I wouldn't mind you being there. To be honest wit you the house hasn't been the same since you left."

"C'mon on, T, don't start."

"Don't start what?" She looked him dead in the eye. "You can't tell me you don't miss being there with us."

"Of course I miss it sometimes. I was wit you for four years and you know how I love Malik."

"Damn, it's like that? You don't love me?"

"I care about you, but you know it ain't like that."

"It's not like that." Trina stood back on one leg in disbelief. "Shit, I can't tell. If it's not like that then why you come over the other night? Why you tell me you love me?! Huh? But it's supposed to be over? Koran, please even you don't believe that shit!"

"Why the fuck you talkin' so loud? I'm not about to do this ole' ignorant ass shit wit you in public," Koran snapped as his cell phone began to ring. "Hold up. Who dis?"

"O just called. They releasing him in an hour," Sheek confirmed.

"A'ight meet me in front of my house in, like, twenty minutes. I'ma hop in the car wit you so we can go pick this nigga up."

"A'ight."

"One," Koran hung up.

"So you just gon' say fuck me, right?" Trina spat, pissed.

"Trina! What the fuck?! I told you I had something to do today."

"How am I supposed to get home?"

"Oh my god," Koran ran his hands down his face. "I told you to drive your own car, but you just had to ride wit me . . . so if you not talkin' about leaving right now, then you gon' have to catch a cab home, flat out."

"Whateva, Koran." She rolled her eyes and waved him off.

"Man, cut that bullshit out." He grabbed her by the arm and made her face him. "Quit actin' like a fuckin' baby. I came wit you, didn't I?"

"Yes."

"A'ight then, well fix yo' fuckin' face? Here." He handed her a stack of one hundred dollar bills. "That's enough for you to get home and for you to buy yourself something. Tell Malik I love him."

"Are you gon' come over for dinner?" Trina called after him with a disappointed look on her face.

"I don't know. I'll call you later and let you know."

CHAPTER TWO

Luv Is U

AZ's "Wanna Be There" played softly from the Alpine speakers inside Sheek's Land Rover. He and Koran sat with the seats tilted back, puffing on a cigarillo stuffed with the finest Dro St. Louis had to offer. Neither man gave a fuck that they were sitting on the police station parking lot waiting on O to come out. Fuck the police. The world was theirs for the taking and nobody, not even the police, was gonna stop them from getting their shine on.

"I wish this dude would hurry up." Koran shifted in his seat to get more comfortable.

"Right, I got shit I need to do," Sheek responded.

"On the real, I wanna smack this nigga. Like, how the fuck he get locked up for five warrants in five different municipalities? What the fuck this nigga be doing? He know what type of shit we on. I schooled him personally on the game. I told him to let his shit bubble on the low and let these other niggas get the name and fame. I ain't got time to be bailing this nigga out for a suspended license and unpaid parking tickets."

"He young. You know how these cats are, man. They don't know shit. They think they can't be touched, especially O. That nigga walk around wit his chest out like he fuckin'. . .Tony Montana or some shit. I'm tellin' you, the boy straight feelin' his self. O be on some wild shit, man. I heard the dude smoke Dips."

"What?" Koran said, surprised by the news.

"Yeah, Rock said every time he see 'em he be on some bugged out shit. He said one night they was at Society, kickin' it, right? And O was actin' a fool. He said the dude bought out the bar, was making it rain, mean mugging niggas, gettin' into it wit 'em over dumb shit. And I know what he speakin' is the truth. 'Cause in the past month alone I've had to check the lil' dude at least twice and you know that's too much talkin' for me. But on the strength of you and that being your man, I haven't cocked the steel on him. But I'm tellin' you . . . that lil' nigga got one more time to test me, B, for real, and it's gon' be some slow singing and flower bringing."

"Like you said, he young so why the fuck you wanna kill the nigga, Sheek?" Koran cracked up. "Yo' ass don't give a fuck. Yo' muthafuckin' grandma could look at you crazy and you would wanna blast her."

"Fuck you, nigga." Sheek couldn't help but laugh, too. "I love my Nana Pearl."

"Wow, okay, enough about Nana Pearl. I'ma holla at the nigga though. Me and him gon' have a one-on-one. O a good dude. He just gotta calm down. He doing too much. All the ice and wavy hair bitches is gettin' to his head."

"Somebody better talk to him—"

"Yoooooo I forgot to tell you," Koran interrupted him, excited.

"Damn, nigga, calm yo' ole' extra happy ass down."

"Check it, guess who I ran into the other day?"

"Who, Tameka?" Sheek chuckled.

"Man, fuck nah." Koran tuned up his face at the thought of her. "If I ever see that crazy bitch I'ma slap the shit outta her."

"Well, who then?"

"Whitney."

"Whitney? I ain't seen her since high school. Where the fuck she come from? Didn't she disappear on you or some shit?"

"Yeah, man, junior year she straight got ghost on me."

"How she look?" "I mean, she was cool when we were coming up, but now that we grown mommy what's up."

"So Whitney that deal?"

"Yeah, I'm on her."

"What about Trina?"

"What about her? When I said it was over I meant it. You know me, I move forward. I never go back."

"Yo, here that nigga is," Sheek said.

Koran and Sheek watched as O came bouncing through the doors as if he hadn't been locked up for the past two weeks. With a confident grin on his face, O made his way over to the car. He was sure to hear a mouth full from Koran, but so what. Whatever Koran had to say would go in one ear and out the other. To O, Koran was an old timer in the game. He didn't get that times had changed. It was okay to stay fly and floss hard. So what if you got locked up? Getting locked up was a part of the game. Any true hustler understood that.

"What up, lil' nigga?" Koran spoke.

"What up?" O replied, getting into the car.

"What took you so long?" Sheek questioned as soon as he got in. "I told yo' punk ass not to have me waiting."

"I had to get my shit. Them hick ass police was tryin' to act like they ain't have my chain."

"Let me see that muthafucka." Koran reached his hand into the backseat.

O proudly passed it to him. He'd spent a pretty penny on the custom-made necklace. The chain was white gold and hanging from it was a diamond encrusted O with a crown on top.

"How much you pay for this country ass shit?" Koran asked, passing it back to him.

"Twenty grand and ain't nothing country about my chain. I get mad compliments."

"That twenty grand could've been in yo' pocket, O."

"I hear what you sayin'. But when you die you can't take twenty grand wit you, so why not blow it on a chain?"

"Yeah, you can't take it wit you when you die, but you sho'll could've had it put up. That twenty grand could've helped get you outta jail. Where the fuck all yo' money going?"

"Shit, I can answer that for you," Sheek chimed in as they hit the highway. "On that bamma ass truck and coon ass chain."

"Whateva, ya'll niggas be hatin'." O's upper lip curled.

He was tired of hearing Koran and Sheek talk shit. What the fuck did they know? Neither of them had touched weight in years. They weren't the ones in the trap day after day, grindin' hard to get money. O and the other niggas on the payroll put food in their mouths. He had the streets on lock. Niggas in the hood respected his gangsta. O was the one putting in all the work. Fuck Koran! It was either get rich or die tryin'.

And yeah, Koran had taught him the game, but his mentoring days were done, finito, finished. O was a man now, not a little boy. He had his own mind and his own set of rules. He could easily venture out and start doing his own thing. Yeah, that's what he would do. Once he got his paper straight O would start his crew.

"O, listen, you know I'm the last one out here to hate. I love the fact that you out here eatin', my nigga. If I didn't want to see you shine I would have never put you on, but you gotta slow down.

These streets don't love you. Don't learn that shit the hard way. I know plenty of niggas who did and guess what—"

"They either dead or in jail," O cut him off. "I know, look man ya'll can drop me off at the pound. I gotta pick up my whip."

O didn't have to say another word. Koran knew when his advice wasn't wanted. O would have to learn on his own that the streets would eat you up and spit you out.

Finding Forever

Computer keys tap danced and phones rang as Whitney sat with her left hand cupping her chin, staring blankly at the door. She should've been busy working on the stack of papers swarming her desk, but that could wait. A week passed by and the fact that Koran hadn't called yet boggled her mind. And, yes, she requested that they be strictly friends, but didn't he long for her taste as much as she longed for his?

Whitney knew that cold November afternoon would come back to haunt her. The right thing to do would've been to say goodbye, but Whitney could never say goodbye to loving Koran. From the moment she laid eyes on him he held the key to her heart, even though, to the universe, he was a street thug. At times Koran could be very cold and vicious, but with her he was always gentle.

Whenever she needed a shoulder to lean on he was there. He was her support system when she felt alone in the world. He gave her permission to be who she was. Before him Whitney never knew a love so strong. She would've given him anything, her heart, her mind, body and soul. She would've swam the deepest seas, climbed the highest mountain, robbed a bank, given him diamonds or pearls, anything except say goodbye.

He was her drug of choice, her forever, the air she breathed. Koran McKnight was one in a million. He was the definition of love and truth. To be loved was to be loved by him. And yes there would be new songs to sing, another fall, another spring, maybe even new lips for her to kiss, but none would compare to him. So until it was her time to leave, Whitney drank up his smile and drowned in his angel eyes. She never thought that years later they would find each other again. She didn't want to deal with the never forgotten, but strategically hidden feelings she harbored for him.

"Why won't this nigga call?" she whispered out loud as her cell phone began to vibrate. "Hello?" she answered on the first ring.

"What you doing?" Koran spoke deep into the phone.

"At work," Whitney answered dryly.

"What's wrong wit you?"

"Nothing, what's up?" she continued in a sarcastic tone.

"I don't like your attitude."

"Yeah, well, I don't like the fact that it's been a week and you're just now callin' me."

"Man, cut that shit out. We talkin' now, ain't we?"

"Yeah."

"Well, a'ight then. Now put a smile on your face and act like you miss me."

"I can't stand you." She finally perked up.

"What you doing tonight? I wanna see you."

"I got plans for a date," she lied.

"Well, tell that nigga you'll see him another day, 'cause you kickin' it wit me tonight."

"How you just gon' tell me what I'm gon' do?" Whitney smirked as her supervisor walked past her desk, giving her the evil eye.

"Fuck, what you talkin' about. I'll see you tonight at Brennan's. Be there by eleven," Koran said sternly before hanging up.

"No this muthafucka didn't." Whitney laughed, hanging up, as well. "I got something for his ass."

FINDING FOREVER

The hit movie, The Chronicles of Narnia, came to mind as Whitney stood before a six-foot medieval style wooden door contemplating her next move. Should she face reality and walk away while she had the chance or take the initiative and enter into a wonderland of possibilities? Plan B suited her much better. Besides, there was no way she was letting her fears get the best of her. She liked the feeling of not knowing what was going to happen next.

"Just play it cool, girl. You're only having drinks," she assured herself as she placed her hand on the knob and pulled.

The atmosphere was ill-lighted and mysterious, but unusually sexy as Whitney crossed over the threshold and headed up the steps. Once she reached the top, a cornucopia of secrets and hidden treasures awaited. The main area of Brennan's, where the bar was located, had a chic Parisian feel to it. The room was lit by soft yellow bulbs while the walls were made of exposed brick. On one side of the room was a huge window overlooking the Central West End. On the other side was a built-in fireplace and fully stocked wine cellar. An assortment of chairs made of different materials and leather benches filled the rustic space.

Whitney searched the crowd of unfamiliar faces and found Koran with a drink in his hand, looking directly at her. Just the sight of him took her breath away. Koran had that masculine thing down to a science. He was boyishly handsome, but there was still something about him that told her he wasn't to be fucked with. He was five-eleven with an athletic build. His style was very current, but edgy. Koran looked absolutely delicious in a Yankee's cap, v-neck tee, black vest and black dirty-wash jeans. Adorning his neck was a beautifully beaded black and silver rosary. To make his cycle complete, he wore a pair of black, gray and white Crea8tive Recreation high top sneakers.

A warm smile exploded onto Whitney's face. The way Koran surveyed her physique with approval as she sauntered over to him let her know that she too looked amazing. Koran couldn't wait to get his hands on her. Whitney was nothing short of hypnotizing in a sleeveless black baby doll dress, fishnet stockings, and leather ankle boots. Loose curls and a pair of dangling gold earrings surrounded her face, highlighted by M.A.C makeup.

"I thought I told you to be here at eleven," Koran chastised her while hugging her tightly. From the glazed overlook in his eyes Whitney could tell he was drunk.

"I'm here now, ain't I?"

"Oh, I see . . . yo' ass tryin' to be grown. Let me tell you something." He pulled her closer so he could whisper in her ear. "Don't make me fuck you up. Daddy don't like when you don't listen."

"Koran, please." Whitney laughed, pushing him playfully in the chest.

"You look nice."

"Thanks."

"Ay, but let me introduce you to a couple of people." Koran escorted her over to where he and his friends were sitting. "This my boy, Sheek, and his gal, Ashley. That's O, Brass, Jay and his girl, Lauren."

"What's up?" Everybody spoke at once.

"Hi." Whitney waved back.

"I know you drinking tonight. What you want me to get you?" Koran asked.

"A Washington Red Apple, please."

"Yo, O, go get my girl a Washington Red Apple."

"Anything you say, boss," the young solider replied in a sarcastic tone.

Whitney could see the hesitation in his body language as he got up and their eyes connected. Unlike the others he seemed to be bored and preoccupied, but when he looked at Whitney a glimmer of lust filtered into his eyes. Everything from the way her hair flowed over her shoulders to the way her dimples glowed in the light had him going.

"I thought you said you were going to get me a drink," Whitney questioned, turning her attention back to Koran.

"I did get you a drink. I had him go get it."

"You're a mess." She grinned, unconsciously wrapping her right arm around his neck and the other around his waist.

"On the real, I'm happy you're here. It feels good to be spending time wit you like this again."

"It feels good to me, too." Whitney eased up and gave him a light kiss on the lips.

"What was that for?"

"'Cause, I missed you."

"Tell me anything," he teased as his cell phone began to vibrate against his hip. Koran checked the screen and saw that it was Trina.

"You ain't gon' answer that?"

"Nah, I'm good." He pressed the end button, sending her call to voice mail.

"Excuse me, sweetheart, here's your drink," O interrupted.

"Thanks."

"Let me know if you need anything else," he stressed, licking his lips.

"Yo, my man, go have a seat. You doing too much." Koran ice grilled him.

"Calm down. I was tryin to help you out."

"Yeah, well, you helped."

Koran wasn't a fool. He was a man and a man knew when his woman was being hit on. A part of him couldn't blame O. If he wasn't with Whitney he would've tried to get on her, too. She was a bad girl. Any man would die to have her, but Whitney was his and only his. If O kept it up he would have to learn that the hard way.

"Koran," Whitney shouted, getting his attention.

"What's up, babe?"

"I know you're not trippin' off that."

"Man please, I'm good," he waved her off. "But hurry up and finish your drink. I'm ready to go."

Five minutes later they left the bar. Outside, Whitney and Koran stood face-to-face, snuggled in each other's arms. There were so many things Koran wanted to say as he took a glimpse into her buttery brown eyes. Whitney was impeccable. There was still so much about her that hadn't been touched, yet so much that he wanted to explore. Fucking around with a nigga like him would only corrupt her life. Yet and still, she was the one he wanted to confess all of his sins to.

"You gon' get a room wit me?" He kissed her lips softly as his cell phone began to vibrate again.

"I don't know, Koran." Whitney released her lips from his and observed the oncoming traffic.

"What I tell you about that?" He turned her face and made her look at him. "I'm right here. Stop running away from me."

"I'm not running."

"Yes you are. You been running for the past eight years, but I ain't letting you get away so easy this time."

"But what if I told you I'm afraid?"

"Don't be. I got you, ma. I ain't going nowhere." Koran examined her face while running his hand through her hair.

Pleased to be in his presence, Whitney stood quiet for a moment. Everything seemed to be perfect. The moon was clearer and more visible than ever. Millions of stars twinkled, cramming the sky. A slight but tranquil breeze filled the air, whizzing over their bodies. Whitney wanted nothing more than to give in to Koran's request, but the memories of what they once shared didn't outweigh her current circumstances. This has to end, Whitney thought while closing her eyes. You can't hurt him again, her conscious reminded her as he massaged her scalp with his fingertips.

Walk away now while you still can. But it was too late. Whitney had already fallen victim to his touch. Koran's mouth and tongue were doing things to her neck that should've been illegal in all fifty states. In a matter of seconds she'd become submerged in his kisses. And, yes, they should take their time before jumping back into things, but nothing had changed. Koran still had a way of getting what he wanted without using force. She was his and he was hers. But Whitney was determined not to fall prey to his sly grin and charming ways.

"It's time for me to go home." She gathered her composure.

"C'mon, ma, come chill wit me."

"Nah, I gotta get up in the morning. I'ma call you though." Whitney quickly pecked his cheek before getting in the car.

Disappointed, Koran inhaled deeply so he wouldn't get mad.

"A'ight, shorty, hit me up tomorrow." He closed her door.

"I will."

FINDING FOREVER

It was six in the morning when Koran tiptoed into the house smelling like Patron. Drunk and high weren't the words to describe how he felt. Koran felt like he was floating on air and, although he was tired as hell, he was determined not to pass out before grabbing something to eat. He was almost sure there was some leftover Lo Mein in the refrigerator. Flicking the kitchen light on he found Trina sitting at the table with her legs crossed. From the look on her face he could tell she was pissed, but all of that was beside the point. Koran wanted to know why the fuck she was up in his crib.

"Where have you been? I've been callin' you all night," Trina hissed.

"Are you conscious? What the fuck are you doing here?" he asked, shocked and confused.

"Evidently I'm here to see you."

"How did you get in?"

"How soon we forget. You gave me a key, dumb ass."

"I ain't gon' be too many more dumb asses and if I gave you a key why you ain't give it back when we broke up?"

"What you think you can just come by my house when you please, but I can't come over here? Koran, please, if you do think that you got life fucked up!"

"Where the fuck is yo' son?" he stressed, throwing his hands up in the air.

"He at Mercedes' house."

"What I tell you about having him over there all the time? You know that bitch got a nasty house."

"He a'ight. Malik know how to call me if something wrong! Now answer the question! Where the fuck have you been?"

"Man, fall back. You better gon' wit that shit. I ain't gotta explain nothing to you." Koran sighed, dropping his keys on the counter.

"I ain't better gon' with nothing! Do you know what time it is? I've been callin' you since twelve o'clock!"

"And?"

"And? Who the fuck you think you talkin' to, Koran? What, you got some other bitch now? That's why you actin' brand new!"

"I'm going to bed," he replied dryly before heading upstairs.

"Nah, don't walk away! It must be true." She grabbed him roughly by the arm.

"Ay." He looked at her like she was crazy and then yanked his arm away. "What I tell you about puttin' yo' hands on me?"

"And what I tell you about tryin' to play me crazy? Keep it, funky nigga! If you fuckin' another chick let a bitch know!"

"Lower your fuckin' voice!"

"I ain't gotta lower shit! Fuck yo' neighbors!" Trina pointed her finger in his face. "I'm tired of you doing me like this!"

"How the fuck am I doing you, Trina? You brought all this shit on yourself. Two months ago you was halfway out the door. You ain't even want to be in a relationship. Up here lettin' them crusty dyke lookin' bitches you hang wit soup yo' head up to cheat. You should've came and talked to me. I would've told you all that nigga wanted to do was fuck. But nah, you thought the grass was greener on the other side. So guess what, ma, I ain't got shit for you."

"So you just gon' keep on throwing that shit up in my face?" Trina rolled her neck as her nostrils flared. "Yeah, I fucked up, but you ain't just gon' deal wit me when you want to! I'm tired of everything being on yo' terms! You just ain't gon' continue to come see me and fuck me when you feel like it!"

"Trina, you cheated on me." Koran placed his hands together as if he was praying. "I ain't never fuck around on you. All I did was try to be a good man for you and a father to Malik. I hit the block daily so you could have your dream house. You wanted the new Z4 BMW, so I copped you one. Them diamonds in your ears came straight from Fred Leighton. You ain't never have to worry about me out here fuckin' some other broad, 'cause every night I was at home dickin' you down. You the one that wanted to fuck and suck another nigga. And not only that . . . you was giving that lame ass muthafucka my money. But you got the nerve to question me? Girl, you better take yo' ass a time out in the corner and think about it."

"You know what Koran? FUCK YOU!" Trina screamed as tears streamed down her face.

"Now you wanna cry? Trina, you got me fucked up. I ain't got time for this shit. You better save them tears for somebody who will wipe 'em," Koran barked, walking away.

"Koran, wait," she begged, taking him by the hand.

"I'm tired. I just wanna go to bed. What is it, Trina?"

"Why can't you just give us one more chance? Please? I'm sorry. I never meant to hurt you."

Trina felt as if her heart was stuck in the center of her throat as she stood and gazed into Koran's eyes. Hours seemed to go by as she awaited his answer. He just had to say he would take her back. She'd learned her lesson. How much longer would she have to beg and plead? If given the opportunity, she was sure to do things differently. She wouldn't take him through unnecessary drama just so she could get her way. She'd love him like he loved her, honestly and truly.

There had to be some love left for her in his heart. They'd been together too many years and shared too many tears for Koran to be done, for real. He just wanted to see her squirm a little bit. Yeah, that had to be it. There was no way Trina was all the way out of his system. Their relationship wasn't over. How could it be when he still came over and made love to her at night?

Trina was willing to do anything to get back what she and Koran had shared. There was no way in hell she was letting him go without a fight. This was her show and, yes, Trina couldn't give two fucks that she was second choice. She'd accepted it from the beginning. She didn't care that she never saw a look of everlasting love in Koran's eyes. That look was for one person and one person only, Whitney. Trina knew all about her and the undying love she and Koran had shared, but that shit was in the past.

Whitney was long gone. Trina was his future and no one was gonna take her place. Koran was a good catch and one hell of a man. She missed his sweet kisses, their long talks at night, and his text messages, asking what she was doing later. Koran accepted her, flaws and all. He took on the role of Daddy when her son's real father neglected his responsibilities.

He took her out of the hood and spoiled her with things she'd only dreamed of. How in the hell could she let all of that go? The thought alone gave her chills. And, yes, her feeling the way she did was all her fault. She'd taken him for granted and thrown their love away on a sexual whim, but who didn't make mistakes? All of her life she'd been in one relationship after another. Trina had never known what it was like to be single and carefree. Koran had to understand that.

Koran couldn't deny that a part of him was still attracted to Trina. Her looks were what attracted him to her in the first place. He used to call her his diamond mommy with slanted eyes. She was five-eight with skin the shade of sweet honey. Almond shaped eyes, a bunny nose and heart shaped lips made up her facial features. To most she resembled R&B singer Monica. And although she had a six-inch waist, Trina possessed more thighs and ass than a little bit.

Koran, being the alpha male he was, thought it wouldn't hurt if he had one more taste of her, so without saying another word he placed his lips on hers and silenced her cries.

Regret would consume him when they awoke, but that was a consequence he was willing to accept. Trina was a beast in the bedroom. She knew just how to please him. The things she did with her tongue made Koran's toes curl. All the chronic in the world couldn't mess with her. Making love to Trina was something he used to enjoy, but tonight was different. There would be no erotic kisses that led from her neck down to the heartbeat of her clit. He wouldn't hold her in his arms until they fell asleep. Trina wasn't getting anything but pure unadulterated, animalistic, non-emotional sex.

Koran was tired of pretending that their relationship was worth holding onto. Too much had been said and done for them to ever go back to the way things were. Trina wasn't worthy of his love anymore. With her back facing his chest, Koran aggressively pulled her skirt up and placed her panties to the side. The lips of Trina's pussy ached from the thought of him entering her.

Bending over she held onto the corners of the kitchen table to stabilize herself.

Koran couldn't wait to dive up in it. The visual of Trina with her legs spread wide open and her fat ass up in the air was turning him on to the fullest. His dick was brick hard, but the days of him fucking Trina without a rubber were over. Koran quickly dug into his back pocket and found a magnum Trojan. Once the condom was securely on he checked to see if Trina was wet by sliding his fingers up and down the center of her slit. Trina was wetter than wet. The tips of Koran's fingers matched the texture of the M.A.C lip gloss she wore.

As he played in her wetness with one hand, Koran placed the other around Trina's mouth. Trina being the freak she was took his index finger inside and began to suck. The room was filled with sounds of her eagerness. It had been weeks since the last time they'd had sex. Trina made a mental note to treasure each stroke as Koran's mammoth dick entered the folds of her lips. The force of the first stroke was heavenly.

Moans of pleasure escaped from Trina's mouth. With her face pressed against the table, she screamed out his name. This only made Koran grind harder. He gripped her waist tight and pounded into her pussy with reckless abandonment. Momentum built with each stroke and with each stroke Trina screamed louder and louder. This was how sex was supposed to be—rough, raw and rugged. She loved every minute of it. Jolts of electricity exploded in her stomach as she felt herself about to cum.

"Ooooooooooooooh, baby, I missed you," she whined.

"Shhhhhhh, be quiet," Koran insisted. He was about to cum and he didn't want Trina distracting him.

"But, baby, I wanna taste it. You gon' let me suck it, daddy? Please let me lick it."

Trina knew she wasn't playing fair. Koran loved receiving head.

There was no way he was turning her request down. Tantalized by the idea of her sucking his dick Koran pulled out. White foamy cream saturated his manhood. Shamelessly Trina positioned herself on her knees. The sight of Koran's ten-inch dick dangling in front of her face made her mouth water.

He had the prettiest dick she'd ever seen. It was thick and rigid. Pre-cum oozed from the tip. Trina made sure to stare up at him with her eyes as she placed him into her mouth. The facial expressions he made were priceless. Trina bobbed her head and French kissed his dick like a pro.

At any moment he was due to explode. The veins in his dick throbbed against the buds of her tongue. Sweat beads dripped from Koran's forehead as she played with her clit. The anticipation of him cumming in her mouth made her suck and rotate her fingers faster. Finally, her wish came true. Semen shot from his dick and into the back of her throat. Trina savored every drop.

As soon as his orgasm subsided and the reality of the situation reentered the picture, Koran began to feel played. Once again he'd fallen into Trina's trap. She threw out the sympathy card, batted her puppy dog eyes and he fell victim. He was stronger than his behavior. The twisted roller coaster ride they were on had to stop. Trina was right; he couldn't just continue to use her body and not want the person that came along with it. After this encounter there would be no more back and forth. This time Koran was gonna cut her off for good.

CHAPTER THREE

Unfinished Business

With his eyes behind shades, Koran sat low inside his old school Cutlass Sierra. The tinted windows were rolled up, giving him the opportunity to see, but not be seen. It was midday, but the corner of Page and Hamilton Streets popped with the sound of bass booming from the trunks of cars passing by. Little children played, but this was an area where even playing was a sport and not recreation.

Kids were trained at a young age to watch out for killers, rapists and thieves. They knew the terrifying sound of gunfire could go off at any second. Page and Hamilton were both streets the ice-cream truck wouldn't dare drive down. Prostitutes as young as sixteen pranced the block in their skimpiest outfits, in search of their next trick. Crackheads roamed the streets feenin' for the ecstasy of their next hit. Graffiti decorated the exterior of buildings that had been vacant for years. Tires, broken bottles, and food wrappings beautified the streets.

It was a sad sight to see, but this area was Koran's territory. It was the place he called home. His little youngins manned the block with a vengeance, distributing bags of crack cocaine. Koran could've encouraged them to stay in school and get good grades. He knew what these streets could do to them over time, but in his mind guidance wasn't the key. These boys had parents and it was their job to raise them, not his.

But on the flipside of things, Koran could feel their plight. At that age he'd had nothing but cashmere thoughts and caviar dreams, too. And just like them, he'd hit the block with no regrets. Koran was gonna get it how he lived by any means necessary and where he lived the only way to get it was to sell ass or sell dope. Koran, being the dude he was, chose the latter. And, yes, he understood that the life he was living was foul, but, no, he wasn't asking God for forgiveness. All he asked was that he be able to live out his dreams until his heart gave out. In his mind that wasn't too much to ask for.

"What up, nigga?" his boy Sheek said, hopping into his car.

"Shit, just checkin' up on things." Koran gave him dap.

"That's what's up. You and shorty get up last night?"

"Nah, I went on home, but, yo, what's up with this cat?"

"Who?" Sheek surveyed his surroundings.

"That nigga, O, man. You see how this nigga lookin'? He on the block in a brand new fit, chain glistening and he got his truck parked right on the corner, like the police ain't watchin'. Yo, I been sittin' here . . . for a minute . . . the police have circled the block twice already. You think they ain't knowing this nigga hustlin'?"

"I told you." Sheek shook his head.

"I mean, what the fuck? I'm happy to see that the nigga is full. Shit, I make sure that all my youngins is eatin', but this nigga trippin'. Never will he be on my corner stuntin' while he sellin' my shit. 'Cause you know who that's gon' draw attention to? Me. And I'll be damn if the boys in blue start runnin' around askin' questions about me."

"I feel you, I feel you. I'ma go handle this shit right now." Sheek opened the passenger side door and got out.

Koran hated to do O in, but the boy had it coming. Out of all the workers, he was Koran's biggest disappointment. He'd taken him under his wing and taught him the game only to be slapped in the face repeatedly with disrespect. There were rules to the game and O wasn't following them. Koran knew why. At first he didn't want to believe it, but O didn't want to take orders from the boss he wanted to be the boss.

He yearned to style and profile. He craved the respect Koran possessed, admired his swagger and loved the attention females gave him. Koran regretted making a conscious decision to ignore the splash of envy in his eyes. If it wasn't for the fact that O was his biggest seller Koran would've gotten rid of him a long time ago.

"Yo, my man, let me holla at you for a second," Sheek said, grabbing O by the back of the neck.

From the inside of the car Koran couldn't tell what was being said, but by the way Sheek manhandled O and the bewildered look on his face, Koran knew his point was getting across. Pleased, Koran started up the engine. Just as he was about to pull off his cell phone began to ring.

"What up?" "What are you doing?"

"Nothing, handling some business." He grinned, happy to hear Whitney's voice. "What's up wit you?"

"Missing you. You miss me?"

"Man, get out of here wit that."

"Ill you mean."

"No I'm not. You already knew the answer to that."

"Umm hmm—"

"Hold up," Koran interrupted her mid-sentence. "My other end clickin'. Hello?"

"You can't call nobody?" Trina asked, trying her best to sound cute.

"I'm on the other end. What's up?"

"I was just callin' to see what was up wit you. I hadn't heard from you in a couple days and plus Malik wanted to talk to you."

"Put him on the phone."

"Malik! Telephone!"

Malik got on the phone. "Koran."

"What up, man?" Koran smiled. Malik wasn't biologically his, but he loved him just the same.

"Nothing, what you doing?"

"Talkin' to you."

"Ah, yeah." Malik laughed. "You know I got a hundred on my spelling test?"

"Nope."

"Mama, why you ain't tell Koran I got a hundred?" Malik took the phone away from his ear.

"I forgot," Koran could hear Trina say in the background as Whitney hung up.

Malik got back on the phone. "Oh, well, yeah, I did."

"I'm proud of you, lil' man. You wanna go to the Mills tomorrow?"

"Oooooh yeah! Can we go go-cart racing?"

"Why not?" Koran chuckled.

"Bet. I can't wait."

"You been taking care of yo' mama?"
"Yeah, but I wish you were here."

"We talked about that, remember?"

"Yeaaaaaaah. I'ma come over to your new house every other weekend. But it's still not the same."

"I know. You love me?"

"You already know the answer to that." Malik giggled.

"You too hip. I love you too, lil' man. Now put ya' mama back on the phone."

"Mama, Koran want you."

"Hello?" Trina said into the phone.

"I'ma be over there tomorrow to come get him."

"Why can't you come over tonight?"

"I got plans."

"What, you going on a date?" she questioned, barely able to breathe.

"I'm not answering that. I told you I had plans."

"Whateva, Koran," she snapped, hanging up.

Any other time Koran would've called her back and cussed her out, but cussing Trina out wasn't worth it. Scrolling through his call list he found Whitney's number and called her back.

"What?" she answered with an attitude.

"My bad."

"You got that right."

"Now what was you saying?"

"I was gon' ask you to have dinner with me later at The Drunken Fish, but now I don't know if I want to. I might call up one of my other tenders, since you actin' funny."

"Ain't nobody actin' funny wit you. You the one playin' games. Had my dick harder than a muthafucka and wouldn't do shit about it."

"Whateva, you'll be alright. So you gon' meet me later or not?"

"You being real tough over the phone. Now when I see you don't let it be a whole 'nother story."

"Koran, please, Joan didn't raise no punk."

"A'ight, Whitney, we gon' see how bad you are."

"I guess we will then," she countered, laughing.

"What time you wanna meet?" he asked, ignoring her last comment.

"Seven will be fine."

"A'ight, I'll check you later then."

"Bye."

"Bye."

FINDING FOREVER

The sun began to set, cascading a pink and orange tint in the sky as Koran stepped out of his silver Audi A8. Koran prepared himself to be cussed out twice in one night as he crossed the street. He was sure Whitney was pissed. It was almost eight o'clock when he left the house and hopped in his car. Trina had made another surprise visit and hounded him from the second she walked through the door. She'd screamed, cussed, threatened, pushed and poked until he couldn't take it anymore. Koran hated to put his hands on her, but Trina was the type of girl you couldn't talk to. He'd warned her numerous times to stop fuckin' wit him and leave, but she just wouldn't listen.

It seemed like the more he reasoned the more irrational she became. When Koran tried to turn on the radio, Trina turned it off. When he tried to enter his closet, she'd block his path. When he hopped out of the shower to retrieve his clothes, they were crumpled up into a ball on the floor. The last straw came when Trina took her hand and mashed him in the back of the head. Koran was livid. Before he knew it he'd turned and slapped her face with so much force she fell to the floor.

Thankfully, Malik wasn't there. Koran would've never been able to forgive himself if he had been. He already felt bad, so bad that he picked Trina up from the floor and held her tightly until she calmed down. Koran didn't want to lead her on by showing her affection, but holding her and saying I'm sorry was the right thing to do. No woman, under any circumstances, deserved to be hit. Koran was raised better. His mother would've turned over in her grave if she knew of his poor behavior.

One thing Koran did know was that things between he and Trina had to change. Neither of them could continue down the path they were going. They couldn't continue to live a lie for the sake of Malik. It wasn't healthy for him or for them.

The Drunken Fish in the Central West End was packed with people. It was hard for Koran to spot Whitney until a mystical cosmic energy guided him in her direction. She was alone, sitting at a table for two with the most adorable pout on her face. Koran couldn't help but stand back and admire her for a second. Whitney was always on point when it came to fashion. Even when they were younger she knew how to put outfits together. She was never the type that had to do a lot to look well, but that day she was more stunning than ever.

Her copper colored skin glistened in the candle light. Whitney's hair was pulled up in a sleek ponytail with one big curl on the end. A small pair of gold star earrings gleamed from her ears. Soft purple eye shadow, bronze blush, and clear lip glass by Bobby Brown decorated her face. On her body she wore a lavender off-the-shoulder mini-dress with side ruffle detail. Her size seven feet arched high in a pair of tan and metallic four-inch peep toe leather heels by L.A.M.B.

"What's up, babe?" Koran wrapped his arm around her neck and kissed her cheek.

"Don't what's up babe me. You're late." She half-heartedly hugged him back.

"I know, I know, my bad. I got caught up."

"Mmm hmm, tell me anything."

"Straight up, did you order?"

"Yeah, I got us some Japanese Chicken Wings and Shrimp Ya-kitori."

"Sounds good, I'm hungry as hell. I ate nothing all day."

"So what took you so long and don't lie?" Whitney asked, taking a sip from her drink.

"I told you, I got caught up."

"So I guess you're not gon' tell me the truth."

"Man, whateva, I am tellin' you the truth."

"Uh huh." She laughed.

"Here's your appetizers," the waitress announced. "What would you like to drink, sir?"

"Let me get a Grand Marnier and pineapple juice."

"I'll be right back."

"This looks good." Whitney rubbed her hands together, excited.

"It does." Koran took a couple of the wings and put them on his plate. "I've never been here before. This is what's up."

"You haven't?"

"Nah."

"This right here," Whitney said, pointing to the Shrimp Yakitori, "Is that deal."

"Nah, this chicken is what's up."

"Let me have some."

"Get one."

"This is good, babe," she agreed, taking a bite.

"Babe? Look at you. I guess you ain't mad at me no more."

"What- and- ever." She giggled.

"Don't front. You know you can't stay mad at me," he said as the waitress placed his drink on the table in front of him.

"How's everything?" the waitress questioned.

"Really good."

"Great. Well, let me know if you need anything."

"Will do," Koran assured her as his cell phone began to vibrate.

It was Trina. Koran sent her call straight to voicemail.

"So Whitney . . . now that it's just me and you and we can finally talk privately . . . tell me . . . why did you really leave?"

"What are you talkin' about? I told you why I left."

"No, you told me the version you wanted me to know, not the truth."

"So now I'm a liar?"

"You said that I didn't. I just know there's more to the story than what you're tellin' me."

"Well, I don't know what more you're lookin' for 'cause I've told you everything."

"So ya'll really just packed up and left because your ole' dude got a job out of state?"

"Yes! What more do you want me to say?" she quipped with an attitude.

"I want you to tell me the truth. Whitney, I know you better than anybody. I know when you not keeping it real."

"Look, I'm tryin' to enjoy my evening wit you. I'm not tryin' to argue," she stressed, frustrated.

"Who's arguing?"

"In a minute we gon' be, so let's just drop it?"

"I don't want to drop it. You owe me some answers."

"I don't owe you shit," Whitney snapped. "As a matter of fact . . . whateva." she waved him off.

"Whateva," Koran repeated in disbelief.

"Nigga, you ain't deaf, yeah, whateva. You know you got a lot of nerve, Koran. First, you come an hour late. Then you badger me about some shit that happened eight years ago. I told you what happened, so if you don't believe me that's on you, 'cause frankly I don't give a fuck," she spat, throwing down her napkin.

Whitney shot him the evil eye, grabbed her purse and left the restaurant, heated. For a second, Koran sat dumbfounded. Did she really just up and leave? he thought. Maybe his aggressive approach was wrong, but, fuck it, he had questions and Whitney was the only person who could answer them. "This broad got me fucked up," he spoke underneath his breath. Leaving enough money on the table to cover the meal and a tip, he got up and followed her outside. With his hands in his pockets, Koran looked to the left in hopes of spotting her, but came up with nothing.

Looking to his right, he caught a glimpse of her dress flowing in the wind as she crossed the street in a hurry. Not willing to lose track of her, Koran looked both ways and ran out into the street despite oncoming traffic. He got a few honks and threats, but he didn't care. He and Whitney had unfinished business. She was halfway to her car when he caught up with her. Taking her by the arm, he grabbed her tightly and pulled her to the side of a building.

"What the fuck is your problem?"

"Koran, let me go." She rolled her eyes, unfazed.

"Fuck nah, you wanna act like a child, I'ma treat you like one!"

"I'm not gon' tell you no more. LET ME GO!"

"WHY THE FUCK YOU KEEP RUNNIN' AWAY FROM ME!"

"I knew this was a bad idea," she said more to herself than to him. "I knew I should've never started back fuckin' wit you. I should've never given you my number. We should've just left the past in the past."

"How the fuck you gon' say some shit like that to me? Especially after all the bullshit you done put me through! Whitney, you left me! I didn't leave you! But you know what? It's all good." Koran licked his lips and backed away. "I'm trippin', we ain't even supposed to be doing all of this, my bad." He turned to walk away.

"So it's like that? You done? You just gon' walk away?"

"Are you conscious?" Koran spun around with an angry look on his face. "Whitney, you just walked away from me! What the fuck more am I supposed to do? I ask you questions, you get offended, so I'm done! You got me up here raising my voice, coming all outside of myself, and that ain't me. So like I said, it's good."

"So you good without me?" She walked up and caressed his face.

"Maaaaaan, this is bullshit." Koran shook his head.

"Nah, tell me . . . are you good without me?"

"Do you know all the bullshit I went through since you left? Half the shit I'm going through right now I wouldn't even be having to go through if you would've stayed yo' ass here like you was supposed to!"

"What stuff?"

"That ain't even none of yo' concern, 'cause remember, you don't give a fuck!"

"I do, Koran, but—"

"But what? What excuse you done came up wit now, Whitney? Huh? 'Cause I ain't for the games, ma. If this ain't where you wanna be then go head!"

"This is where I wanna be," she spoke softly as her lips brushed up against his. "You know that."

"Then why you keep taking me through all of this unnecessary bullshit?"

"Shhhhhhh, just be quiet."

Whitney was fully aware that she would regret the decision she was making later, but in that moment everything was how it should be. Koran had taken control and pinned her against the wall. Whitney couldn't escape him, nor did she want to. To be in his embrace was heaven. She felt so small.

For a brief moment they gazed into each other's eyes, secretly praying that the feeling arising in each of their souls would never fade. Koran missed the way her skin tasted, the way his tongue flicked against it while they made love. Kissing her neck, he bit softly, causing her mouth to release moans of pleasure. He could feel her heartbeat pound against his broad chest as he unzipped his pants.

A look of excitement danced across Whitney's face. Closing her eyes, she wrapped her arms around his back and held on tightly as he placed his hands on her butt and lifted her up. A wonderment of pain and indulgence seeped through Whitney's body as her skin scraped against the rough surface of the brick wall. Gasping for air, she held on tightly and wrapped her legs around his back, allowing him access to her hidden treasure.

Immediately, the overwhelming sensation of his dick being suffocated took Koran's manhood as he entered Whitney slowly. She was so tight his heart sank to his feet. Tears filled the brim of Whitney's eyes as he rocked inside her at an unhurried pace. This was making love, the pure definition of it. What they were creating was crazy black magic. Neither cared that someone could walk by and see them. This moment had been predestined in time. Sweet, sticky cream covered Koran's dick as he thrust himself deeper and deeper. Whitney wanted to scream. Her back arched so high it felt as if her breasts were pressed up against the moon. Koran was exploring crevices that were unknown. The folds of her pussy ached. The faster he pumped the wetter she became.

An orgasm was approaching. This feeling hadn't come over her in years. The sensation was blinding. Finally, she was letting go of everything. All of her fears and doubts were now being thrown to the wind. With Koran was where she wanted to be. His long strokes had her in a daze. Hot cum dripped down from her walls, saturating his dick. He was cumming, too. Neither cared that he'd exploded inside of her. All that mattered was the moment and that they were back together.

"I love you," she admitted, opening her eyes.

"I know you do."

FINDING FOREVER

The song "Bed" by J. Holiday came to mind as Koran lay on his back, enjoying the sunlight as it peeked through the blinds. Whitney lay on her side, nestled securely under his arm. Her naked body kept him warm and that was how it had been all night. For hours, they'd made love with the light from the moon as their guide. Their encounter was so intense it seemed as if it was their first time. After cumming numerous times, Whitney finally lost consciousness and drifted off to sleep.

Koran couldn't even join her. Trina blew up his phone the entire night. His voicemail was full of hysterical rants and raves. He wondered how he was gonna tell Whitney about Trina and Malik. They'd come so far, but once he revealed his secret everything would change. She was sure to leave him, this time maybe for good. Koran didn't want to chance that. He couldn't lose her twice. It would kill him.

Yet telling the truth was the right thing to do. Whitney deserved nothing less. Koran looked down into her solemn sleeping face and grinned. Her beauty was irreplaceable. He could watch her sleep forever. She looked so at peace. The sheets rested comfortably, covering the lower half of her body leaving her top exposed. Just the sight of her perky brown breasts made his dick hard. Koran wanted nothing more than to suck each nipple until her back arched and she moaned his name. A smile suddenly appeared on her face, causing her dimples to shine like the sun. He wondered what she was dreaming about. He hoped it was of him.

Koran checked the clock. Twenty minutes had passed. He

didn't want to leave, but he had to go soon. Koran never broke a promise, especially not the ones he made to Malik. He'd never done it before and he wasn't going to start now, despite his feelings for Whitney.

"Good morning, sleepyhead," he said, ruffling her hair.

"Hi," Whitney covered her mouth in case her breath stank.

"Yeah, you might wanna go and handle that," he teased.

"For real?" Her eyes grew wide.

"Yeah, 'cause that smell is all bad."

"Oh my god." Whitney rushed to get up.

"I'm just fuckin' wit you, ma." Koran cracked up laughing.

"You get on my nerves." She hit him in the chest.

"Nah, for real, I need to talk to you about something."

"About what?" Whitney pulled the covers over her. "Is it something serious?"

"Yeah, but you gotta promise you won't get mad."

"If it's something bad I am going to get mad, so let's just not talk about it. I don't wanna hear any bad news right now."

"I understand that, but it's important."

"Baby, please," Whitney cooed, stroking his cheek. "Let's just enjoy each other's company. We haven't been like this in years. Why spoil it?"

Koran sat for a second and contemplated whether or not he should spill his guts and risk hurting his and Whitney's relationship or keep quiet until the time was right. Koran decided that seeing Whitney smile was better than seeing her upset, so he kept his mouth shut.

"A'ight, shorty, but I did want to tell you this Saturday a bunch of us are going to Nectar. I would pick you up, but I got some things I need to handle, so invite one of your girls and I'll meet you there."

"You know I'll be there." Whitney rested her head on his shoulder and ran her fingers through the hair on his chest.

Koran had the sickest physique. His skin was the perfect shade of copper, which highlighted his carefully crafted pecks. Whitney traced his nipples with her fingertips and then made a trail down to the six-pack of muscles covering his abdomen. They were like small mountain peaks. Naughty fantasies of her tongue replacing her finger clouded her mind. Her mouth watered from the thought. Flashes from the night before caused bolts of fire to explode in the pit of her stomach.

Whitney missed his thrust, the way his hips wound in a circular motion. She ached for the way sweat beads dripped from him and onto her body like hot lava. She liked the bittersweet taste of his penis. Visions of it as it slid from between her breasts and into her mouth flashed before her eyes. It was time for round five. She hoped he was up for the fight 'cause Whitney still had a couple of rounds left in her.

"Baby," she purred, straddling him.

"What?"

"You know what." Whitney bit into her bottom lip as she took his dick in her hands.

"I gotta get up outta here."

"I know, but just one more time." She eased down and licked the tip.

"You don't fight fair." Koran closed his eyes.

"You're right . . . I fight to win," she replied before slipping his entire dick into her mouth.

CHAPTER FOUR

Damaged

Afternoon approached as Koran placed his key into the knob and turned. To his surprise Trina wasn't in the kitchen or living room waiting on him. The coast was clear. Maybe for once he could spend some time with Malik without her being all up in his face. Koran made his way upstairs. The sound of the Disney Channel's hit show, The Suite Life of Zach and Cody, blared from Malik's room. He could hear him clack his toy men together as if they were at war. Opening Malik's door, he peeked his head through.

Malik didn't even notice him standing there. He was too busy pretending. Koran did everything in his power not to laugh. Malik looked a hot mess. He had on the smallest set of pajamas Koran had ever seen. The long sleeve button-up shirt with trains on it squeezed his plump belly tightly. Some of the buttons were missing and the ones that were still holding on were in the wrong holes. The pants were a whole other story. They were royal blue and made of thermal material, which meant they hugged his thighs and butt tightly. On top of that they were flooding, but Malik loved them. He was unwilling to let them go. They were his favorite pair.

"Why you not dressed?" Koran spoke after composing himself.

"Mama told me not to put on my clothes until you got here." Malik stopped playing, not missing a beat. "Where you been?"

"You nosey, stay out my business."

"Just tell me."

"Out, why?"

"'Cause mama been lookin' for you."

"Where she at?"

"In the room."

"Mama's eyes were red again. I think she was up crying all night. Did ya'll have another fight?"

"Nah."

"Well, why was she crying?"

"I don't know. She probably just got something in her eye. Now, did you eat?" Koran quickly changed the subject.

"Yeah, I got up and fixed me a bowl of cereal. What, you want some? 'Cause I can fix you a bowl. You know we got Golden Grahams downstairs."

"I'm good, but thanks."

"That's what's up? So what you get me?" Malik asked not taking his eyes off the television.

"You bold. How you figure I got you something?" Koran scrunched up his face.

"Why we always gotta go through this? Will you just give me my present?"

"Man, me and you gon' box." Koran opened the door wider so he could toss Malik a bag.

"I knew you got me something!"

"Yeah, I stopped by the game store."

"Oooooh, you got me Dragon Ball Z and NBA Street! Thanks Koran!" Malik ran over and hugged him around the waist.

"You know I got you, but let me go holla at ya' mama. Get

dressed while we talkin', a'ight?"

"Okay," Malik responded, half-listening. He was already plugging in his GameCube.

Koran closed Malik's door and made his way across the hall to what used to be his and Trina's bedroom. Inhaling deeply, he turned the knob and entered. Koran's old bedroom was outstandingly lavish. Trina had done her thing when she put everything together. The wall behind the king-sized bed was black and there were two black and white family photos exposed by recessed lighting above the headboard.

Koran loved his old bed. It wasn't too soft or too hard. It was just right. A total of nine pillows adorned the ivory and white satin sheets, and matching nightstands and lamps stood on each side. A charcoal gray couch with an array of throw pillows sat in front of the bed and a wooden coffee table finished off the room.

Trina usually kept everything neat and clean, but today things were dramatically different. It looked as if a tornado had blown through. All the pillows were slit open, feathers covered the floor and the lamps were broken. Old photos of he and Trina were cut into a million pieces, the sheets were ripped and the mattress had been turned over. The clothes and shoes Koran still kept there had been thrown all over the place.

Rushing into the bathroom, he saw the words, Fuck You! Sincerely, Trina, written on the mirror in red lipstick. All of Koran's male toiletries, including his Anthony Logistics shaving cream, lotion and shower gel had been squirted into the sink. Koran didn't want to believe his eyes. The only thing still in one piece was Trina, who was fully dressed and sitting with her legs crossed on the couch. A freshly lit cigarette rested between her index and middle fingers as she exhaled smoke rings from her mouth.

Trina was determined to remind him that she was that bitch. If they were going to go heads up she was going to do it in style. Trina was the shit in a black and white rayon poncho, black camisole and black booty shorts. In her ears, she rocked her favorite pair of Chanel logo earrings and on her feet she sported a pair of black Giuseppe heels. Trina's shoulder-length hair was flat ironed bone-straight with a part in the middle.

Homegirl didn't know where to start first. A part of her wanted to be rational, but in a situation like the one she and Koran were in being rational wasn't an option. She wanted to slap the shit out of him. She wanted to cuss and scream. She wanted to spit in his face. Trina could feel her nails scraping his skin. Yes, she'd fucked up, but that didn't mean he was going to disrespect her and get away with it.

More then anything, Trina's ego was bruised. She honestly didn't think Koran had it in him to move on. He had her fucked up if he thought she was gonna let him go that easily. She'd been in the picture way too long for it to be over. And, no, Trina didn't necessarily want Koran and Koran only. Frankly, she could do without him if she absolutely had to. What she couldn't do without was the house, the money and the cars. She loved the street fame that came along with being his girl. There was no way in hell she was giving up the chinchilla furs and VVS stones.

"So this how we doing it now? You ignore my phone calls?" she questioned calmly, never taking her eyes off the television screen.

Placing his keys into his pocket, Koran shook his head. He was beside himself with rage. Koran didn't know how much more he could take. Trina was pushing him closer and closer to his breaking point. With his head down low, he walked over to the couch and stood before her.

"Trina, what the fuck is yo' problem?"

"Who is she? Just tell me her name."

"I'm not tellin' you shit."

"Then why won't you answer none of my calls?"

"I don't have to answer your calls when you call me. What is it that you don't understand? We not together no more and frankly I can't keep on doing this shit wit you. This shit is tiring, man."

Trina sat speechless. She felt empty inside. All the words she'd rehearsed overnight escaped her memory now that she and Koran were face-to-face. It didn't matter anyway. Nothing she said or did was gonna convince him that with her was where he needed to be. Trina wanted to scream so loudly the heavens could hear. The idea of being alone was too much for her to bear.

Koran had to see the tears filling the brim of her eyes. Didn't he feel her pain and despair? How was she supposed to sleep at night when he wasn't lying by her side? Every time the phone rang she prayed it was him. Koran was supposed to love her forever, so why wasn't she good enough now?

"I ain't tryin' to hurt yo' feelings or nothing, but I don't love you no more."

"Don't tell me you love that bitch already? Please don't."

"As a matter of fact, I do."

"This is some bullshit! I fuck up once and now it's over? What about all the shit you did to me? Yo' ass ain't perfect!"

"I never said I was! What I said is that I don't want to be wit you!"

"You ain't gotta be wit me! Fuck you! Don't nobody need you!"

"You fuckin' crazy." Koran shook his head.

"Now I'm crazy 'cause you fuckin' another bitch? Where you

take her last night, Koran? Did ya'll go eat?! Huh?! Where'd you take her? Was it Lucas Park Grille or Red?"

"Since you wanna be smart, it was The Drunken Fish."

"Cheap but cute," Trina scoffed, lighting up another cigarette. "I don't even know why I'm trippin'. The bitch you fuckin' probably ain't nothing but a Reebok broad."

"You right, Trina, just like you was when I met you."

"Fuck you! 'Cause if you think you leavin' me you got another think coming. 'Cause . . . I . . . ain't . . . going . . .nowhere!"

"I don't wanna be wit you no more! What the fuck about that can't you understand? Stop seeing what you wanna see and get that shit through that big ass head of yours?"

"You think I care about you not wanting to be wit me? It ain't about us, Koran! It's about Malik! You know you the only daddy he knows! How you think that makes him feel, knowing me and you ain't together no more?"

"I understand that." Koran clapped his hands together. "But us arguing everyday like we do is not that deal! Half the time I don't even like being around you."

"So being wit me is that bad?"

"Trina, at first it was all good, but I ain't there wit you no more. I've moved on."

"So that's it? It's over? You don't even wanna try no more?" Trina's bottom lip quivered.

"I don't know what more you want me to say, T. I've said everything. I told you how I feel, but you gotta accept it."

"How can I accept it when I still love you? I don't wanna be wit nobody else. All I see is you." She held her stomach and cried.

"But you got to. We can't keep doing this shit, man. You gotta get yourself together for you and Malik. He don't need to see you carrying on like this. That shit ain't cool, man."

"I know, but it just hurts so bad. I need you back, baby. I can't take this pain." She cupped his face in her hands. "Just please come back home. I'll do anything you tell me to. Just come back." Trina wrapped her arms around his neck and hugged him tightly. "Please, just love me like I love you?"

Once again Koran didn't want to lead Trina on by showing her affection, but holding her was the right thing to do.

"You know I can't do that." He hugged her back. "I'm just not there no more."

"There's gotta be something I can do," she sobbed.

"Look, you gotta pull yourself together." Koran wiped her eyes. "I'm sorry for puttin' my hands on you."

"I'm sorry for messing up your stuff. I just didn't know what else to do to get your attention. I love you, Koran. I just wish you could see that."

"Mama, are you okay?" Malik asked, entering the room.

"Yes, baby, go on back in your room." Trina finished wiping her face so her son wouldn't see that she'd been crying.

"Yo' mama cool, man, she just having a bad day."

"Well, will ya'll stop arguing, please?" Malik pleaded.

"Anything for you, lil' man," Koran assured, taking him by the hand. "C'mon so you can finish getting dressed."

"We still going to the mall?" Malik sniffled.

"Nah, we gon' go to the Loop."

"Can Mama go?"

"Yeah, yo' mama can go," Koran reluctantly replied.

FINDING FOREVER

Tribal drumbeats filled the air as Koran, Malik and Trina stepped out of the car. It was a beautiful, sunny Saturday afternoon. Children and their parents lined the sidewalks and watched as a group of musicians played various percussion instruments. A juggler, face-painter and hoola-hoop dancer accompanied them. Malik was instantly excited.

The smile on his face made Koran even happier. Malik's happiness was what mattered most. If he and Trina could get on the same page about that, then everything would be okay. Koran looked over at her. She seemed at peace as she danced around in a circle with Malik. When Trina was calm her entire being lit up. He just wished she'd stay that way. The new overly emotional Trina was not at all attractive.

"Koran, look at Mama! She hoola-hoopin'!" Malik shrilled in delight.

"I see her, man," Koran replied as his cell phone began to ring. "What's up, future?" he answered, stepping off to one side so Trina wouldn't hear his conversation.

"Nothing, what you doing?" Whitney giggled, feeling like a school girl.

Even though she wasn't right next to him, Trina could tell by Koran's body language that he was on the phone with another woman. The grin that stretched a mile wide across his face confirmed it.

"Chillin' wit my peoples, that's about it," Koran told half the truth. "What you doing?"

"Nothing, I ain't been feeling good all day."

"What's wrong wit you?"

"I've been really tired all day and my knees ache. I guess I'm about to come on."

"Yeah, it's about that time."

"Look at you, keeping up with my period." Whitney chuckled.

"Gotta make sure everything is everything."

"Well, look I don't want to hold you up. I was just checkin' in wit you, seeing what was up. I miss you."

"Is that right?"

"Yeah."

"I miss you, too. I'ma hit you up later, a'ight?"

"A'ight."

"One." Koran flipped his phone shut.

It took everything in Trina to suppress the grin her mouth so desperately wanted to form. She was more than pleased with the fact that Koran rushed to get off the phone with his mystery woman. Maybe she still had a shot, after all. Whoever this chick was she couldn't be that important. If Trina continued to play her cards right she'd have Koran back in the palm of her hand in no time.

Finding Forever

Dolla's smash hit, "Who The Fuck is That?" echoed out of Nectar's door and into the streets. Koran was hyped as hell. This was his element. A perfect combination of arrogance and confidence enhanced his swag. Koran couldn't help but laugh at all the clown ass niggas that gawked as he pulled up in front of the club.

His whip game was sick. That night he pushed his baby, a champagne colored Ashton Martin DBS. The car was every man's fantasy. Koran felt like James Bond as he popped open the door and stepped out into the cool night air. He could see the haters admiring his outfit. As always, he was fresh to death in a fitted black Gucci jacket, black v-neck tee, dirty wash jeans and Gucci sneakers. Covering his locs was an all black LA cap. The only pieces of jewelry he wore were a diamond stud in his ear and an Audemer Piguet watch on his wrist. Koran was that dude. There was no denying it, but to him this was just another day in the life of a boss.

A fresh line up and a brand new fit was nothing to him. Koran always looked good and smelled even better. He couldn't wait to get inside and do his thing. All week he'd been anticipating getting out and partying. Plus, the fact that Whitney was inside waiting on him excited him even more. The two hadn't seen each other since the night of their erotic encounter in the Central West End. Koran thought keeping his distance was best. Until he figured things out he didn't want to lie to Whitney any more than he had to.

"FAM," Koran heard a familiar voice say. In front of the building was the birthday boy, Sheek. "What took you so long to get here?"

"C'mon, you know how I do. I never step out the house if my shit ain't all the way right." Koran smiled, running his hands over his face and clothes.

"Nigga, please."

"I know you ain't hatin'?"

"Picture that, but, ay, where your girl at? I thought you said she was coming," Sheek asked as they made their way to the door.

"Why you worried about my girl?"

"I'm just tryin' to make sure you straight, 'cause I don't wanna hear none of that bitch ass complaining tonight. It's my birthday. I ain't for no bullshit. I'm tryin' to kick it."

"You got me fucked up. My girl in there chillin' dog."

"A'ight then, that's what's up, c'mon."

The atmosphere inside Nectar was poppin'. If St. Louis had a red light district this would be it. The interior design was off the meter. Hanging from the ceiling was an assortment of lantern lights that doused the room with a seedy scarlet hue. The hypnotic glow of amber-shaded lamps also filled the many spaces and angles of the room. Lush curtains covered the windows. In the center of the dance floor was a two-sided diamond shaped bar. Right next to the entryway was a private balcony. Red and black leather couches and benches amplified the space.

"Damn, this muthafucka packed," Koran admitted, surveying the spot.

"It's always like this on Saturdays."

"I'm gon' have to come here more often."

"Yo, ain't that yo' girl over there?" Sheek pointed across the room.

Sure enough Whitney was on the dance floor with her hands up in the air, grooving to Glenn Lewis's, "Back for More." The reggae-inspired beat complimented her seductive moves. Whitney was a beast when it came to dancing. She could wind her hips with the best of them and when she dropped down low it made Koran want her even more. All the women in the spot were scantily clad in sexy outfits but, Whitney stood out the most. The black jersey tank dress she wore clung to her curves. The hem stopped midway down her thigh, accentuating her ballerina like legs and Scorah Pattullo heels.

Koran couldn't take his eyes off her. The way she twisted and twirled had his dick harder than a jawbreaker. His tongue couldn't wait to savor her skin with sensual kisses. He couldn't take it. The environment was hot and sticky like her cream when she came. Fuck waiting until they got home, he wanted to make love in the club.

Koran was just about to make his way over to her when he noticed O step in behind her. Shocked, he played the background and peeped the scene for a second. Whitney didn't even know he was behind her as she slithered her way up from the floor. A look of surprise burst onto her face when her butt pressed up against his hard dick.

Whitney quickly turned around. Once she recognized it was O she playfully hit him on the chest, then continued to dance. Koran was disappointed. He expected her to walk away. O, on the other hand, seemed to be quite pleased with himself. His hands roamed freely down the sides of Whitney's waist as her booty popped and bounced. Heated, Koran made his way through the club. Not in the mood for pleasantries, he bo-guarded his way between Whitney and O.

"Hi, baby," she gleefully smiled, wrapping her arms around his neck.

"What's up wit you?" Koran took her by the waist and turned around so he could get a good view of O. "I got this, homeboy."

"My bad, I was just keepin' it warm for you," O responded with a smirk on his face. He was drunk.

"Oh, that's how you feel?" Koran got in his face and pressed his forehead up against his.

"Koran, calm down," Whitney begged, tugging on his shoulder.

"Man, you better tell this lil' nigga. I don't know what type of shit he on, but he got me fucked up, for real."

"Straight, it's like that, Koran? It's like that? After all the shit we been through?" O challenged.

"Fuck the shit we been through! It's about right now and right now you on some homo shit!"

"Homo? Homo? Nigga, you callin' me gay?" O tilted his neck and extended his left ear in disbelief of what he'd just heard.

"I ain't call you gay! I said you on some gay shit, now what you wanna do about it?" Koran challenged.

"Koran, baby, please stop! It's not even that serious." Whitney tried her best to calm him down.

"Koran, chill out." Sheek pulled him back.

"Fuck that shit, Sheek, cuz! This nigga foul!"

"You know I'm the last one to stick up for that nigga, but look at him! He drunk, man! He on that shit!"

Breathing heavily, Koran took a glance at O and saw that he was high and pissy drunk, but that shit didn't matter. Everybody knew being drunk only made your true colors shine through.

"Man, come here." He grabbed Whitney by the arm and dragged her across the room. "What the fuck was that shit about?"

"What shit? What did I do?" she asked, baffled.

"Don't play dumb, ma, it's not a good look on you."

"Whoa." Whitney released her arm from his grasp and stepped back. "Have you lost your fuckin' mind? Who are you talkin' to and what is your problem?"

"Why the fuck you let that nigga rub all on you like you some kind of ho?"

"A ho? Are you kidding me? We were just dancing."

"It looked like more than dancing to me."

"Please do not tell me you're jealous?"

"Don't come to me wit that jealous bullshit. I ain't no mutha-fuckin' female."

"Well, get that bitch up outta you and act like it," Whitney joked to ease the tension.

"Man, you got me fucked up." Koran's upper lip curled.

"Whateva, if you gon' be actin' crazy I'ma leave," she retorted, stepping past him.

"Don't play wit me. What I tell you about runnin'?" He grabbed her hand to stop her from leaving.

"Ain't nobody playin' wit you. You the one starting wit me."

"My bad, come here." Koran pulled her close. "Just do me a favor. Stay away from that nigga. O on some shady shit right now."

"That's all you had to say. And if you ever call me a ho again I swear on everything I love it's gon' be me and you."

"You think you tough, don't you?"

"Let's just put it like this. I ain't no punk."

"Whateva, you look nice though." Koran eased up and mellowed out.

"'Bout time you noticed." Whitney's face brightened with a smile.

"You gon' give me some tonight?"

"I don't know. I'll think about it," she smirked.

"A'ight, that's what's up. This muthafucka the shit, ain't it?"

"Yeah, I like it. This gon' have to be our new chill spot."

"Right," Koran agreed, really not listening.

Whitney was rambling on, but his eyes were glued to her hips and thighs. Koran wanted nothing more than to dip off and find a spot that was made just for two.

"Koran, are you listening?" she asked.

"Yeah."

"Mmm hmm, then what I just say?"

"I don't know. Quit askin' me so many questions." He laughed.

"I knew yo' ass wasn't listening." She playfully hit his chest before wrapping her arms around his neck. "What you got your mind on?"

"You."

"Oh, really?" She licked her bottom lip.

"Yeah, I wanna see what you got on underneath this little bitty ass dress." Koran slid his hand up her thigh.

"Absolutely nothing," she answered with a look of lust in her eyes.

"You must be tryin' to get fucked." He stepped forward so her back could rest against the wall.

"You ain't know?"

"Oh, I see . . . somebody wanna be grown. You wanna be a big girl today, huh?"

"I've been grown, sweetie," Whitney challenged.

"Let's see how grown you are when I pull my dick out and stick it up in you."

"Koran, please."

"What, you think I won't?"

"I know you won't."

Before Whitney knew it she had been spun around. Her breasts and hands were firmly pressed up against the wall causing her back to arch and her butt to stick out. Koran had never seen anything sexier. The expression on her face was priceless. Whitney had a look of fear, surprise and anticipation on her face. Stepping up behind her, Koran ran his hand through the hair at the back of her head.

He knew she could feel his hard on. Whitney, being the freak she was, adjusted her butt so his dick was in line with her pussy. Turning her head, she looked over her shoulder and gave him a look that said, "I dare you."

Koran never backed down from a challenge. Without hesitation, he surveyed the club to make sure no one was looking and unzipped his pants. Whitney released a startled gasp when she felt his hard dick slap the skin between her thighs and hit the lips of her pussy. Immediately, she became wet.

"Koran, what are you doing?" Her voice quivered as he played with her clit.

"Shhhhhhhh," he ordered. "You only get five strokes, okay?"

"Okay." Whitney closed her eyes and relished the sensation of his dick entering the slit of her wet pussy.

"And when I'm done don't be beggin' for more."

"Alright," she moaned.

"One." Koran moved his hips as if they were slow grinding.

"Two."

"Three," Whitney joined in, enjoying their freaky game.

"You wanna play?" he questioned, stepping back and then pounding into her hard. "Four."

"Koran," she squealed, ready to cum.

"Be quiet. Five." He gripped her waist tightly and pumped even harder.

"Just one more stroke, daddy, please?" Whitney begged.

"Nope." Koran grinned, placing his dick back into his pants. "Wait until we get home."

"Are you serious?"

"Yep."

"I can't believe you gon' play me like that. I was just about to cum."

"Deal wit it. I told you, you was only gettin' five strokes."

"I can't stand you. Now I'ma be walkin' around wit a wet ass all night."

"You wanna go home?" Koran pulled out a Black N' Mild and lit it.

"Nah, I'll be back."

"Where you going?"

"To the bathroom, so I can freshen up."

"Hurry back."

"I will."

While he waited for Whitney to come back, Koran inhaled smoke from the Black N' Mild and surveyed the crowd. The party was crunk. People were enjoying themselves as they drank, danced or mingled. He could see O upstairs, leaning up against the rail with a salty look on his face. His man was whispering something in his ear, making him even madder as they both mean mugged Koran. Koran wanted his pot'nah to amp him up to do something drastic. If he jumped Koran was sure to put something in him that he'd never forget.

"You cool?" Sheek came over and wrapped his arm around his shoulder. "You straight?"

"I'm good. You enjoying yourself, birthday boy?"

"Yeah, I'm about to cut this cake in a minute, but before I do I'ma pop that bottle of Perrier Jouet you gave me. I know you gon' take a sip."

"Hell yeah, I'ma get a glass. You know how much that bottle cost me?" Koran joked.

"Well, bring yo' punk pussy ass on then."

"Give me a second. I'm waiting on Whitney to come back from the bathroom."

"A'ight, we up top." Sheek walked off.

As Sheek disappeared into the crowd, Koran scanned the club for Whitney. He couldn't spot her anywhere. Where is this girl at? he wondered, checking his watch. She'd been gone over ten minutes. It didn't take that long to use the bathroom. Koran made his way through the club in search of her. Halfway across the room, he noticed that O was no longer standing where he once was. This set off an alarm in Koran's head. Instantly, he knew something foul was up. Koran walked even faster. Pushing his way through the mob of people, he spotted O with his arm around Whitney's waist. His hand cupped her chin as he tried his best to force her to kiss him. Whitney struggled to get away, but his grip was too tight.

"O, get off of me," she yelled.

"Why you trippin'? We was just chillin' a minute ago. Just give me one kiss. I know you want to."

"I don't want to do shit! Get the fuck off of me before I scream and if I scream Koran gon' come over here and whoop yo' ass!"

"FUCK KORAN! SCREAM! I DON'T GIVE A FUCK! THAT NIGGA AIN'T GON' DO SHIT!"

Koran could feel his blood pressure rise. This was the last straw. Grabbing a hold to the back of O's shirt, Koran spun him around. A look of bewilderment filled O's face as Koran's fist slammed repeatedly into his face. O never even had a chance to fight back. All of the rage and frustration Koran had kept pent-up inside was being released on him. Whitney had never seen Koran in such a state. She wanted to scream for him to stop, but she was too scared. Koran's punches were coming at lightening speed. Before O knew it, he was on the floor, curled up in a fetal position and begging for help.

"Get yo' bitch ass up," Koran barked, kicking him in the face.

He'd completely blacked out and gone to another place. Koran kind of liked the state he was in. Each kick that connected with O's ribs lifted Koran's spirit more and more. He was tired of trying to do right by everybody. What did being good get you, anyway? The people in his life that he tried to treat right in turn treated him like shit, including Whitney.

She'd left without so much as a goodbye when he needed her most. His mother preferred shooting up over taking care of him. For four years Trina had played with his love and money for her own selfish needs. O mistook his guidance and friendship as a sign of weakness. Wherever Koran turned, evil haunted him, so instead of running from it he now embraced it.

Whitney's eyes bulged at the sight of blood spewing from O's nose and mouth. Something had taken over Koran. She could see it in his eyes. He wasn't the same. A dark cloud hovered over him and Whitney didn't want any part of it. Slowly, she stepped back. Out of the corner of his eye, Koran could see her about to walk away. This enraged him even more. Just as he was about to pull his gun and finish the job, Sheek and three security guards approached. It took all three of them to pull him off of O. Security had to drag Koran out of the club, he was so riled up. Once he'd calmed down security finally let him go.

"What the fuck is wrong wit you?" Sheek questioned. "You been wildin' out since you got here."

"Cuz, that nigga had his hands all over Whitney!"

"For real?"

"Yeah, up there talkin' about fuck Koran! On everything I love I will kill that nigga!" Koran paced back and forth.

"All of that ain't even necessary. His ass just off the payroll, plain and simple, but where is Whitney?" Sheek looked around.

"I guess her ass left!"

"Why she leave?"

"Shit if I know. Where the fuck is my phone?" Koran patted his jacket pockets. "Give me a second, cuz," he said, walking away.

After locating his phone, he dialed Whitney's number.

"Hello?" she answered after several rings.

"Where the fuck you at?"

"Koran, don't call my phone talkin' crazy."

"So that's how it is? I get into it wit a nigga and you bounce?"

"You damn right!" she spat. "I ain't got time for that ghetto bullshit and neither should you! You're twenty-five years old and still fightin' in the club! That shit ain't cool! You know how wack you look?"

"I'm far from wack and I was protecting yo' ass!"

"Okay, Koran, but did you have to beat him like that? You were about to kill him."

"So? He shouldn't have been disrespecting me."

"Listen to how you sound right now. You sound like a fuckin' idiot! If this the type of shit you gon' be on I swear to god I will go down to the muthafuckin' clinic tomorrow and terminate this pregnancy! 'Cause I don't have the time, nor the patience to be worried about you out here in these streets beefin' wit some nigga over some bullshit! I expect more from you and I most definitely expect more from my child's father!" she yelled before hanging up.

Koran was speechless. For a minute he stood and gazed at the ground in a daze. Whitney was pregnant with his baby. Nothing in life could be better. He wanted to jump for joy, but the fact that she still didn't know about Malik and Trina loomed in the air. Shit was getting more and more complicated by the minute. Koran had to confess and soon.

CHAPTER FIVE

Da Baddest Bitch

"Nothin' make a women feel better . . . then Berettas, and Amarettos, button leathers and mad cheddars . . . chillin' in the Benz wit my amigos . . . tryin' to stick a nigga for his pesos," Trina sang as she exited the highway in a cherry red CLK. There was no stopping her hustle. She was determined to stay fresher than the next bitch. Like vinegar and oil, she and females didn't mix. Chicks were too conniving. The first chance a ho got she would try to crack for Koran's bank, so fuck a friend. The 380 inside her Prada bag was all the company she needed.

Trina was determined to stay laced in diamonds and pearls. And, yeah, she could work a nine-to-five, but fuck a job. She cashed checks on a regular at the bank of Koran. After her mental breakdown, Koran felt more sorrier than ever for her. Every other day he was stopping by to check up on her and Malik. They'd even spent some time together without arguing. Things were finally going Trina's way. It was just a matter of time before they were back together.

After parking her car in the garage, Trina made her way inside West County Mall. Her first stop was Nordstrom's. A pair of pink Salvatore Ferragamo heels was screaming her name. It didn't matter that she'd already spent well over three grand. Trina had money to burn. Switching her hips like a top model, she entered the shoe section like the diva she was. A sales attendant instantly rushed her way.

"May I help you?"

"Yes, can I see those pink Ferragamo heels in a size nine?" Trina pointed to the shoes she was talking about.

"Sure, anything else?"

"Umm, yes, let me . . . also see . . . those brown Marc Jacob Gladiator sandals and those logo Coach sneakers."

"I'll be right back."

Trina removed her shades and took a seat. While she waited she saw O and a girl browsing around.

"O," she called out.

"What's up, T? Hold up, babe, give me a minute," O told the girl he was with.

"How you doing, baby girl? You look good." He hugged Trina.

"I'm good. I haven't seen you in a minute. How's everything been going?"

"You tell me?" O took off his Gucci glasses.

"What happened to your eye?"

"Oh, you don't know?"

"Know what?"

"Me and ya man got into it last night at the club."

"Got into for what? From what I knew you and Koran were cool."

"I thought so too, but I guess ya man didn't like the fact that I was callin' him out on his shit."

"What you call him out on?"

"Yo, this ain't none of my business or nothing, but ya boy been doing you mad wrong, T, and just on the strength that me and you came up together I feel as if you should know."

"Know what?"

"I mean, you probably already know that nigga be out here doing his thing. But shit wit him and this new chick is crazy. Every time we go out she around. Yo, on the real I think the nigga might be in love."

"Oh, really? What's her name?"

"Whitney."

"Whitney," Trina repeated as her heart skipped a beat. "Are you sure?"

"Yeah. What, you know her?" "Nah, not personally." The wheels in Trina's mind began to turn.

"I mean, Koran got a good thing going on wit you, T. It ain't right that he out here doing you wrong like that."

"I agree." Trina sucked her teeth. "Koran needs to be taught a lesson."

FINDING FOREVER

It was the first day of summer. The best time to fall in love. Whitney and Koran lay basking in the sun on top of a blanket in the park. London, Whitney's rottweiler, sat next to them. Live jazz music serenaded them as they lay on their backs playing with each other's hands. Tree branches swayed gracefully in the wind. The sweet aroma of barbeque filled the air. Joggers jogged while children of all different persuasions played gleefully in the grass. It was the perfect summer day.

"I'm sorry about last night," Koran apologized.

"I know you are," Whitney replied, intertwining their hands. "Just don't let it happen again."

"I won't."

"You better not," she challenged.

"Okay, Whitney, that's enough."

"It's never enough." She jumped up and began to playfully beat him up.

"So now you a tough guy?" Koran took her by the wrist and pinned her down.

"Why you gotta pin me down? Why you can't fight fair?" Whitney wrestled to regain control.

"Fuck fightin' fare, I play to win."

"Uh-huh, wait until I get up. I'ma whoop yo' ass." She laughed so hard her stomach hurt.

"Yeah . . . no!" Koran cracked up laughing as London began to bark.

"Okay, baby, I'm done playin'. Let me up."

"Nah, don't punk out now. You wanted to fight, so fight."

"For real, baby, let me up," Whitney screamed, feeling sick. Everything around her was spinning, including the earth.

"Nope, not until you kiss the guns." Koran placed his bicep up to her lip.

"Koran, stop! I'm not playin'," she yelled, pushing him off.

"Damn, baby, what you push me for? We was just playin'."

"But when I tell you stop, stop," she shouted, holding her head. London was still growling, which got on her nerves even more. "London, shut up!"

"You a'ight? Is it the baby?"

"No, I'm not okay!"

"Ay, you know I don't play that. Lower your fuckin' voice," Koran said sternly.

"Stop cursing at me! I don't feel good." She lay down.

"Well, come here and quit actin' crazy." Koran pulled her close. "Now what's wrong? You gotta boo-boo or do you want to go to the hospital?"

"Quit playin' so much. I was dizzy."

"When you go to the doctor?"

"Next Thursday."

"Well, I'ma go wit you." He kissed her forehead.

"Okay."

"You okay now?"

"Yeah."

"You sure?"

"Yes," Whitney replied annoyed.

"Yo, ma, be easy. All I asked you was a question."

For a while an uncomfortable silence filled the air. It wasn't like Whitney to pop off with an attitude for nothing. She didn't think he saw it, but Koran peeped the distance in her eyes. It always seemed like Whitney was there physically, but her mind was someplace else. Koran wished she'd tell him what was up so they could fix whatever problem she faced, together.

"I'm sorry for snapping at you."

"You good, but let me tell you one thing. Don't you ever in yo' fuckin' life drop no important shit like that on me again and hang up. That shit ain't cool. We better than that."

"I know. I'm sorry. I was wrong. It's just that sometimes I get so frustrated with you. This whole drug dealing lifestyle is just so not me. I mean you are too smart for all that hood shit. You could be doing so much more wit yourself. Like, remember we were supposed to go to college together. You were gonna study business so you could open up your own chain of stores in the neighborhood."

"I still want to, but—"

"But what? It's never too late to follow your dreams, Koran. You can take some online courses. I'll even help you register."

"We'll see what's up."

"See, you on that bullshit. For real, Koran, if you don't listen to anything else I say, listen to me now." She sat up.

"Look at you. Got your serious face on and everything," he teased.

"I'm not playin'. I'm for real. You've lost track of your goals, boo. Selling dope was only supposed to be a temporary thing so you could get yourself financially stable after your mother died. Now look . . . it's eight years later and you still doing the shit."

"I hear what you sayin', but I've had a good run, ma. I just can't let that shit go."

"You call living your life the way you do a good run? Koran, be for real. Take a step back and honestly look at what the game has done for you. As far as I know you've been locked up twice and both times you had to sit down for a minute. You're always on the go. You don't get any sleep. You're constantly watching your back. You've been shot and shot at numerous times. Niggas is out here threatening your life. I mean, come on. Who wants to live that way? Koran, you could be making the same amount of money you're making now the legal way and without all the fear and the constant struggle for supremacy. You're better than this game and I know deep down inside you want better for yourself."

"I feel you. You're right. The money been so good that it kinda clouded a nigga's judgment. The end was never supposed to justify the means. I guess somewhere along the line I lost sight of that. But, I mean, I can't even front. Yo' boy like to floss."

"And there's nothing wrong wit that. Everybody likes to look good and feel good about themselves, but you don't have to risk your life and participate in killing others to do so. I mean, we got a baby on the way and I ain't tryin' to burn bread or nothing, but you and I both know that nobody stays on top forever. Sooner or later you either gon' get knocked or killed, 'cause somebody gon' end up catching feelings and start hating."

"Goddamn, why you have to go and get all deep on a nigga? I hate it when yo' ass is right."

"'Cause you needed to hear it. Somebody got to knock some sense into your head and since your mother is not here to do it, I will."

"That's what's up."

"She didn't want you to live your life in the fast lane like she did. She wanted more for you. Hell, I want more for you, 'cause I know you have it in you to do something great. No, scratch that, extraordinary."

"I'ma give what you said some thought."

"Please do, 'cause you never know how long you're gonna live. I don't want you to wake up ten years from now and realize it's too late."

FINDING FOREVER

After spending the entire day with Whitney, Koran made his way over to Trina's to see Malik. As he pulled up to the house he noticed an unfamiliar car in the driveway. To make matters worse the car was parked in his spot. Koran had to park his truck on the street, which he hated. He figured that the car belonged to one of Trina's chickenhead friends. All he knew was they better not be in his house drinking and smoking.

He'd told her on more than one occasion to do that shit outside of the house. Malik didn't need to see his mother prancing around drunk and high. Koran went to put his key in the lock, but to his surprise the door was unlocked. Confused, he entered the house to find some man he'd never seen before on the couch with his feet up watching television. What fucked Koran up even more was that the dude was dressed in nothing but a wife beater, boxers and socks. On top of that, he was sipping on Koran's last Boulevard Wheat Beer.

"Who the fuck are you?" Koran asked, pulling out his gun.

"Koran . . . you're home," Trina sneered, coming around the corner dressed in nothing but a pink Victoria's Secret robe.

"Here you go, baby, eat up." She handed the guy a plate of macaroni and cheese, cabbage, chicken and cornbread. "Koran, this is Richard. Richard, this is Koran."

"Trina, what the fuck is going on? You ain't tell me you had a man," Richard said, looking nervous as hell. He looked like he was about to piss in his pants.

"Where the fuck Malik at?" Koran's chest heaved up and down. It was taking everything in him to keep his composure and not shoot both of them.

"Upstairs." Trina looked him square in the eye and arched an eyebrow.

"My bad, dude, shit. I ain't know she had a man and this was yo' house. I wouldn't disrespect another man's crib like that, real talk." Richard got up and slowly reached for his pants.

"Boy, sit down. You ain't gotta go nowhere," Trina insisted. "This is my house. My name is on the deed. Ain't that right, Koran?"

Koran gazed into her eyes. He was hoping to see some kind of fear or regret beneath the surface, but nothing was there. Cocking her neck, Trina gave him a look that said, "I dare you to do something." And Koran did just that. Before either of them knew it his left hand was wrapped around Trina's neck. Koran tried to squeeze the life out of her.

Trina tried to scream, but her cries for help weren't allowed to rise in her throat. Instead, she hit and kicked. Koran felt her punches, but they were like pebbles being thrown into a lake. Trina was no match for him. He could see her face turning blue. The veins in her neck bulged beneath his hand. Dribbles of spit rolled from the corners of her mouth as she tried to pry his fingers away. Koran heard his inner-voice telling him to stop before things went too far, but hadn't they already? Let her go, man, his conscious told him as his grip became tighter. She's meaningless. Everything in Koran wanted to kill her, but Trina wasn't worth a life sentence in prison, so he let her go.

"I hate you," she coughed, holding her throat.

"You hate me, Trina? Just the other day you was saying how much you love me."

"Fuck you!"

"A'ight, I'm outta here." Richard attempted to leave.

"Ain't nobody going nowhere." Koran raised his arm and pointed his gun in Richard's direction.

"Man, I ain't even know. I ain't tryin' to get in no beef like that." Richard threw his hands up.

"Nigga, put yo' hands down! I ain't the police! You good! Just listen to what I have to say." Koran grabbed Richard by the head and spoke into his ear. "I don't give a fuck what ya'll do! You can fuck that ho until her pussy bleed . . . eat, shit and sleep, but you won't do it up in this muthafucka! And yo' ole trifling ass..." He turned and eyed Trina. "...done gave this nigga my beer. MY LAST FUCKIN' BEER!" Koran grabbed the almost empty bottle and threw it against the wall.

The sound of glass exploding popped in the air. Pieces of glass flew everywhere.

"Damn, Koran, what's the problem? Was it me fuckin' another nigga in yo' crib or was it him drinkin' yo' beer?"

"I don't give a fuck about you fuckin' some other nigga, Trina! You're a whore, a fuckin' bird! Any nigga wit a lil' bit of cash can get that! But let me tell you something," Koran yoked her up by the neck. "You got me fucked up if you think you gon' get away wit this shit! I never once . . . in the four years we were together cheated on you, bitch!"

"Well, maybe you should have!"

"I'ma gon' and head out, 'cause ya'll got a lot to talk about." Richard tried to leave again.

"Nah, dog, you cool. Go on and have a seat." Koran cut him off.

"Nah, I think I'ma head out."

"You know what?" Koran stopped to think. "You probably right. That would be the best idea for both of us. Now where was I? Oh yeah, this shit is over, you understand? Me and you is a wrap. I'ma look out for Malik . . .but, bitch. . .yo' nasty ass on your own."

"Nigga, we don't need you! You ain't Malik muthafuckin' daddy, no way! And fuck what you talkin' about! This shit between me and you been over! As a matter of fact, we was never really in a relationship! Walkin' around here thinkin' you king-ding-a-ling! Don't you know when you being used? I guess not, stupid muthafucka! Get yo' hands off of me!" Hurt, Trina pushed his hand away.

"You know what, Koran? You're weak! You's a punk...ass...nigga! You think you the shit just 'cause you sell a little weight! You ain't Frank White! The shit you push ain't nothing but a misdemeanor, nigga!"

This bitch is crazy, Koran thought as he stood speechless.

"That's right, nigga! Stand there and look stupid! I wish I never met your sorry ass! And I dare you to put yo' hands on me again! 'Cause if you do I'ma call the police and they gon' come and lock yo' BLACK ASS UP!"

Koran never backed down from a challenge. Every fiber in his being wanted to knock the shit out of Trina. Visions of him pounding her head into the floor flooded his mind. He wanted her to taste blood. Koran wanted her to feel his pain. Why did she hate him so much, yet for the past four years claim she loved him so?

"On everything I love, I could fuckin' kill you right now."

"Yeah, yeah, yeah, save that shit you talkin' for the next bitch."

"Since you got that slick ass mouth and wanna have other niggas in MY crib, yo' ass need to find yo' own place so you can have all the niggas you want and do whatever it is you wanna do up in that muthafucka!"

"Negro please, my name is on the deed, so I don't gotta go nowhere!"

"Oh, you gettin' yo' ass up outta here one way or another!"

"Alright." She grinned. "If you want me gon' so bad then you go and tell Malik that we gotta go! 'Cause I ain't tellin' him shit!"

"You a fuckin' idiot," Koran barked as he turned to find Malik standing at the top of the stairs in tears.

"Koran, please don't make me leave! I wanna stay," he wailed.

"Come here, lil' man." Koran met him at the bottom of the stairs and picked him up.

"I don't wanna leave, Koran! I promise me and Mama will be good!"

"It ain't even about that, man. Me and your mama dealing wit grown people stuff."

"Then why can't I just come live wit you?"

"Maybe you can." Koran looked over his shoulder and shot Trina a look.

"That shit ain't even happening." She stepped in and took Malik from Koran's arms. "Listen to Mommy, Malik. Koran don't want us here no more. He don't love us."

"But Koran we're sorry! Mama won't be mean no more. Just please let us stay!" Malik begged.

Koran didn't know what to do. The right thing would've been to stick to his guns and demand that Trina go, but the miserable look on Malik's face tore him up inside. It was a known fact that the love Koran held in his heart for Malik stretched as wide as countries and was as deep as oceans. He hated to see him in pain, especially when he was the cause of it.

"You ain't gotta go nowhere, lil' man." Koran wiped Malik's face and kissed his cheek.

"That's what I thought." Trina sucked her teeth.

"You promise?" Malik asked to make sure.

"I promise. Yo' mama's right. This is her crib. I can't put her out, but I can quit taking care of her. Her new man got that responsibility now." Koran smiled with a devilish look on his face.

"First off, I don't even know that nigga like that! And I don't need no nigga to take care of me!"

"That's what's up, Trina, do you. Malik, I'ma holla at you later."

"But I wanna go wit you."

"Nah, stay here wit ya mama, okay?"

"Okay." Malik held his head down.

"Chunk the deuce, nigga?" Trina quipped with her hand on her hip as he slammed the door behind him. "I hope this nigga don't think it's over 'cause if he do he got another think coming."

FINDING FOREVER

Rain drops the size of gumballs fell from the sky as strikes of thunder echoed loudly into the atmosphere. It was one of those nights when Whitney found it difficult to sleep. For hours she'd tossed and turned under the sheets. A feeling of helplessness consumed her. She hated the way darkness overtook her room. All she wanted was to rest, but her mind wouldn't stop thinking.

It didn't matter which way she turned; songs, ideas and fears kept choking her mind. She wanted to scream, she was so frustrated. She wished Koran was there. Being in his presence always put her at ease. Now more than ever, she needed his support. There were so many things she needed to say. Painful secrets plagued her soul. She wondered how he'd react if he knew of all the important things she'd neglected to say.

Sitting up, Whitney bent her knees up to her chest. The rain was driving her crazy. Screams of rage saturated her chest. She had to escape. Where was Koran?

At that moment she needed him to save her from herself. He was the only one who could dry her tears. Somebody had to be her strength. Whitney was just about to pick up the phone when there was a faint knock at the door. Her prince charming, her lover, her angel was finally there. Whitney ran as fast as she could, but the door seemed so far away. After what seemed like an eternity they were finally face-to-face. Whitney could breathe again, at least for a while.

"Hey, what's wrong?" Koran questioned as she rushed into his arms.

"Nothing, I just missed you, that's all."

"I missed you, too." He brushed her hair back and kissed her gently on the forehead.

"What are you doing here?"

"Man, it's a long story. I don't even wanna talk about it." He let her go and stepped into the house.

"Okay." Whitney closed the door, perplexed. "You hungry?"

"Nah, I'm straight. All I wanna do is lay down. You gon' lay down wit me?" Koran extended his hand to her.

"Yeah." She smiled.

Koran led them both into her bedroom. Once in bed, he lay behind her with his hand resting on her stomach. A slight grin crossed his face as he remembered that their baby would be born in November. A baby girl that looked just like Whitney would be the best gift she could ever give him. As they lay bathing in the essence of one another, Whitney closed her eyes and thanked God for blessing her with the man she hoped to one day call her husband.

"You ain't gon' never leave me, are you?" he asked out of no-where.

"Why you ask me that?" Whitney placed her hand on top of his.

"Just answer the question."

"No, I'm not gon' leave you. What, you planning on leaving me?"

"Picture that."

"Well, stop askin' me crazy questions then."

"And don't think I'm on no sucka shit, but just lay down wit me until I fall asleep, a'ight? It's been a long night." Koran sighed.

"You sure you don't want to talk about it?"

"Yeah, I'm good as long as I'm here wit you."

"I feel the same way." Whitney placed a loving kiss on the back of his hand. "I feel the same way."

CHAPTER SIX

U, Me & She

"Come on out, babe." Koran leaned against the wall with his arms and legs crossed.

"I can't believe you got me doing this dumb shit!" Whitney yelled through the bathroom door.

"Quit writing checks ya ass can't cash, then! Now bring yo' sexy ass on! I'm hungry, my dick hard and I want some pussy!"

"Don't get stupid." Whitney swung the door open.

Koran's eyes bulged at the sight of her. Whitney looked sexy as hell in a black lace halter bra and matching rhinestone trimmed g-string. Her luscious breasts spilled from the barely there cups. Koran couldn't wait to get his hands on them, but first she had work to do.

"You hot. . .but you still gotta go in there and fix me some Alfredo."

"You're an idiot. You're really gonna make me cook in my lingerie?"

"You lost the bet, ma. We said that if you lost at spades you had to cook naked. But since you wanted to whine and complain, me being the nice guy I am, I let you put on some panties and a bra."

"I'm gon' get you back for this." Whitney rolled her eyes and turned around.

"Get yo' ass in there and cook." Koran slapped her hard on the butt.

"Oww, nigga, that hurt." she winced holding her butt cheek.

"You'll be a'ight."

"Do you want chicken and shrimp in the pasta?"

"Hell, yeah." Koran brought a chair into the kitchen and sat down.

"So you're gonna sit there and watch me cook, too?" Whitney questioned as she filled a huge pot with water.

"Duh, that was the plan."

"I can't stand you."

The melodic sounds of Dwele drifted from the living room into the kitchen as Whitney switched around the kitchen in five-inch stiletto heels. Koran couldn't take his eyes off her butt. The plumpness of her ass was ridiculous. With each step, her booty bounced and jiggled. Whitney was the epitome of what a real woman should look like.

She wasn't skeleton skinny or outrageously obese. Whitney was thick, plain and simple. Koran drowned in her presence each time they were together. As the water began to boil, Whitney stood over the stove sautéing the Cajun flavored shrimp. The aroma in the kitchen was off the chain. Koran's stomach growled, he was so hungry. What he didn't know was if he was hungry for food or for Whitney, because both enticed his senses. Koran walked up behind her and wrapped his arms around her waist. Whitney felt so small in his embrace.

"You gon' let me get some?"

"You know you don't have to ask."

Koran quickly spun her around. Her lips barely touched his. He could see her chest heave up and down in anticipation. Whitney's nipples were so hard they felt like needles prickling his pecks. A manifestation of desire consumed Koran as Whitney's luscious pink lips assaulted his neck with tender sweet kisses. Flashbacks of her tongue tickling the tip of his dick overpowered his mind. He wanted her to suck it so badly. The mere thought made his penis stand at attention.

"Somebody's hard." Whitney smirked with a hint of lust in her eyes as she slowly lowered herself into a squatting position.

She yearned for the decadent taste of his manhood in her mouth. Koran's dick was like a caramel sensation. Whitney wrapped her lips around the tip and pulled him in inch by inch until the tip reached the back of her throat. Koran couldn't take it when she deep throated his dick. Even if he wanted to he couldn't stifle his groans. Koran's moans ignited a fire in the pit of Whitney's stomach. Overcome with desire, she sucked harder and faster. Whitney had an insatiable appetite for dick. She could hardly compose herself.

She loved the way Koran's penis slid in and out of her mouth with ease. Sucking dick alone could make her cum. The faster she stroked the more Koran's knees wanted to buckle. Not wanting to cum yet, he stepped back. Nothing had to be said. Whitney already knew what was up. Koran wanted to taste the kitty.

She wanted him too. Her pussy longed for a good tongue-fucking. With both her thighs in his arms, Koran placed Whitney onto the countertop. In one swift pull he removed her g-string. Whitney was already dripping wet. Koran bent down so his face was parallel with her slit. Using his index and middle finger, he opened up her lips. Like a rose bud, she blossomed. The pink flesh of Whitney's pussy drove him insane.

"You think you deserve this?" he asked before lightly licking the folds of her lips.

"Yes, I've been a good girl, daddy." Whitney moaned, spreading her legs wider.

Koran was meticulously swirling his tongue around the bud of her clit, causing it to rise and fall in his mouth.

"I'm so wet, daddy." She arched her back as sparks of adrenaline shot through her pelvis.

"You want this dick?" Koran gently bit her pussy lips, then licked her clit.

"Yeeeeees."

"You want it real bad?"

"I want it real bad!"

"So what you want me to do?" He tongue kissed her clit and played in her wetness.

"Oooooooh, daddy, why you doing this to me?" she shrieked, massaging the top of his head.

"Don't be shy, tell a nigga what you want."

"I want you to bend me over—"

"And, what?" he questioned plunging his fingers in and out.

"Fuck me real hard, until I cum all over yo' dick."

Whitney's freaky words were all Koran needed to hear. Pulsating with desire, he gripped her waist and picked her up. He could feel her body whispering how desperately she needed him as he led her to the bedroom. Gently, he laid her on her back. Whitney watched intently with her index finger in her mouth as he undressed.

Koran's physique resembled an African warrior's. Muscles rippled throughout his chest and arms like ocean waves. Whitney's pussy ached with anticipation for him to enter her. She wanted nothing more than to taste him on her tongue. Naked, Koran made his way over to the bed.

Fire roared in his eyes as he placed sweet kisses down her neck. With each of her breasts in his hands, Koran proceeded to tease her mountain peaks with his mouth and tongue. Whitney responded with a soft, "Mmmmmmmmm." She was so enthralled with passion she didn't even realize that her stomach had met with the sheets.

Going with the flow, she arched her back and prepared herself for him to enter her wet slit doggy-style. Koran didn't even have to check. Her shaking thighs let him know she was ready. An hour later they lay spent in each other's arms. The food had burned, but neither of them cared. What they'd just created was far better than any food they could've eaten.

FINDING FOREVER

A look of denial mixed with fear graced Whitney's face as she made her way back into the waiting area of Dr. Chancellor's office. This can't be happening again, she thought, but a part of her had felt it coming. A part of her had died in a matter of seconds. Her body was numb. So many questions and concerns plagued her mind that she didn't even hear the receptionist call her name.

"Ma'am?" One of the other patients tapped her shoulder, causing her to jump. "The receptionist is talking to you."

Whitney blinked her eyes profusely and tried to regain control. She was stronger than her circumstances. She'd gotten through this before.

"Thank you." She half-heartedly smiled.

"Okay, Whitney, we're gonna need you back in here immediately," Pam urged with an expression of concern on her face.

"Okay." Whitney nodded incoherently.

"I'm so sorry, Whitney, but if it's any consolation I know you're happy you're having a girl. Despite what's going on, you and Koran should still try and celebrate that fact."

"Mmm-hmm." Whitney choked back the tears that were trying to slide down her cheeks.

Whitney didn't yet know it, but her day was about to get even worse. Over in the corner with her legs crossed flipping through a magazine was Trina. After hearing the names Whitney and Koran the magazine was no longer of interest to her. This can't be that bitch, Trina thought, sizing her up. She had no idea Koran had a baby on the way.

Jealousy and hate shot through her veins as she watched Whitney stand with her belly poking out. If Koran thought he was gonna go on with his life as if the time he and Trina had shared didn't exist, he had another think coming. Trina had one more trick up her sleeve and now was the perfect time to use it. Whitney was halfway out the door before she caught up with her.

"Excuse me." Trina tapped her shoulder.

"Yes?" Whitney turned around.

"Is your name Whitney?"

"Yeah, who wants to know?" Whitney looked her up and down.

"Koran's wife."

Unable to speak, Whitney held her breath and looked at Trina like she was a crazy person. This had to be a dream or, better yet, a nightmare. There was no way a person could get this much bad news in one day.

"Say that again." Whitney cocked her neck so she could hear her better.

"No need for me to repeat myself. You heard me correctly, but let me tell you something. I don't know what this isyou and him got going on, but I ain't going nowhere. Me and Koran been together four years and we got a son together, so I would advise you to step the fuck off, 'cause Koran is mine."

With her head down, Whitney shook her head and licked her bottom lip. If she wasn't pregnant she would've knocked the shit out of Trina for approaching her with some bullshit.

"You know what, ma?" She chuckled. "You caught me on the right fuckin' day."

With that said, Whitney shot Trina a look and walked away.

"Trina Lewis," the nurse called.

"I'll be right there," she answered, picking up her purse with a sinister grin on her face.

Finding Forever

Later on that night, Koran entered the house to find Whitney sitting alone on the couch with his favorite red fleece blanket draped over her body. The only light that shined throughout her loft was the blaring light from the television screen. Koran could smell trouble in the air. The stoned look on Whitney's face spoke volumes. Usually when he came in at night she'd speak or run into his arms for a hug, but tonight was different.

Whitney didn't even look his way. Her eyes stayed glued to the program as if he wasn't even there. If she did look at him she'd hurl. His presence alone made her stomach queasy with disgust. Before asking her what her problem was Koran thought back on what he could have possibly done wrong. He'd taken out the trash like she asked. He hadn't forgotten to clean out the tub after bathing. It wasn't her birthday or some other major holiday.

Whiney hadn't called him all day so he knew he hadn't missed any of her phone calls. Wait a minute, a thought crossed his mind. Fuck, I forgot to call and ask her how her doctor's appointment went. Koran immediately felt horrible. How he could forget something so important was beyond him.

"Yo, my bad, babe. I forgot." He sat down next to her and placed his arm around her shoulder. "How the doctor's appointment go? My baby doing a'ight?"

Whitney didn't respond. She couldn't, due to the fact that she was boiling with anger on the inside. If she spoke to him she would explode, so instead, she held her tongue and focused on the television.

"Yo, you hear me? How the appointment go?" he asked again while rubbing her hair.

Whitney jerked her head away and still wouldn't respond.

"So that's how it is? You just gon' ignore me and watch television? Is it really that serious?"

Whitney inhaled deeply and tried her best to pretend he wasn't even there.

"What is you huffing and puffing for? I said I was sorry. Damn, my bad. You know I had to be hella busy to forget something like that, so you need to stop with the attitude and get yo' shit together quick, before you fuck around and make me mad."

Whitney slowly turned and looked him in the face. Everything in her at that very moment wanted to slap the shit out of him. She could vividly see her fist slamming into his face and him wincing in pain. How dare he be so selfish and rude after the day she'd been through?

"Now you just gon' stare at me?" Koran eyeballed her back with an attitude. "I said I was sorry. I ain't gon' keep on apologizing."

Whitney crossed her arms over her chest, licked her lips and laughed. This muthafucka got some nerve, she thought.

"Man, what the fuck is wrong wit you? What is yo' problem?" Koran barked, fed up.

"You're my fuckin' problem," Whitney snapped.

"Are you conscious? Who the fuck are you talkin' to? I ain't did shit to you!" Koran pulled his arm from around her and looked at her like she had lost her mind.

"Is that how you talk to Trina and Malik when you mad?" she shot back.

For a second everything around them went silent. Koran was shocked. "What?" he finally asked.

Whitney didn't even reply. She simply shot him a look that said, "You heard what I said."

"What you talkin' about?" Koran played dumb.

How in the fuck do she know about Trina and Malik? he wondered, terrified. Koran's worst nightmare was becoming a reality right before his eyes. There had to be a way out though. He could lie to her, but Whitney was too smart for that. Knowing her, she probably already knew the truth. He could always start an argument and turn things around on her and make her feel guilty, but Koran couldn't do that. Even if he wanted to he didn't have it in him to do Whitney that way. He loved her and valued her feelings too much.

"Baby, listen . . . look." He took her hand and held it tightly. "I wanted to tell you, but I ain't know how. You know what I'm sayin' . . . but it ain't nothing like that. I stopped fuckin' wit her before you even came back into the picture. The only reason I still deal wit her is because I take care of her lil' son. Now I don't know who told you what, but I'm tellin' you . . . me and Trina been a done deal. On the real, the bitch is crazy. If It wasn't for Malik I would'a been had somebody chop her fuckin' head off."

Unfazed by his too little too late confession, Whitney threw the blanket off of her and got up. She could honestly care less about what Koran had to say. His words were like leaves blowing in the wind. Besides, she had bigger things to worry about. If he did have another girlfriend, then so be it. The other bitch could have him as far as she was concerned.

Whitney entered the kitchen, flicked the light on and proceeded to find ingredients to make herself something to eat. Koran was dumb heated. Did this chick really just get up and leave like I wasn't talkin' to her? he thought with his mouth wide open. This had to be some cruel joke the universe was playing on him. There was no way his beautiful, sweet Whitney could be treating him this way. She was always so giving and understanding, so why now was all of that being thrown out of the window? Koran had to make her see that whatever she'd heard was completely untrue, so he too got up.

"Whitney, you hear me?" he pleaded, following behind her. "I don't fuck wit her, straight up. You know I'm not even on no shit like that. Me and her don't even talk. When I call there I ask to speak to Mal and that's it."

This nigga just don't get it, Whitney thought as she placed slices of fresh deli meat onto a piece of bread. Shaking her head, Whitney yawned and rolled her eyes as she stepped around Koran and put away the bread.

"Yo, quit playin' wit me." He grabbed her arm tightly.

Without saying a word, Whitney took one look into Koran's eyes and he let her go.

"My bad, I'm trippin'. I ain't mean to put my hands on you. I just wish you would listen."

A part of Whitney wanted to hear him out, but she just couldn't. Her heart was too raw to digest anything he had to say, so instead, she picked up her plate, which consisted of a sandwich, chips and a pickle and went back into the living room. Never in life had Koran felt more helpless. Nothing was as it should be. Nothing he said or did mattered. It seemed as if Whitney was slipping away before his very eyes.

This wasn't how their relationship was supposed to be. They were supposed to be happy and celebrating the birth of their unborn baby, but now everything was fucked up and Koran might have just lost the love of his life forever. As Whitney sat on the couch Indian style, she realized that her meal wasn't as appetizing as she thought it would be. Every bite tasted like sand.

At that point all she really wanted to do was curl up underneath the covers and go to sleep. Maybe then she'd wake up and all her troubles would be gone. It was hard enough to face her own reality, but having to deal with Koran's deceit was only making life worse.

"Okay, ma, look, I know I fucked up. I know I did . . . but I never meant to hurt you. For years I never thought I would see you again, but look we here, we back together. We gettin' ready to have a baby and you don't even have to tell me. I already know it's a girl. But guess what? She gon' have big brown eyes and deep dimples just like you." Silent tears raced down Whitney's cheeks as Koran held her in his arms.

"We building a life together, ma, so why would I want to fuck that up? I ain't tryin' to be wit nobody else but you. You my heart. I love you and I promise if you let me, I'ma do everything I can to make this shit up to you."

The mention of them building a life together caused Whitney to cry even harder. If only Koran knew what she was going through? The pain in her heart stung like a bee stings. Whitney was drowning and Koran didn't even see it. This time he wouldn't be able to save her. Only one person could and Whitney wasn't sure if this time he would.

CHAPTER SEVEN

I'm With U

After hours of Whitney crying hysterically and Koran not fully knowing why, they both got into bed and drifted off to sleep. The next morning Koran lay flat on his back, knocked out in only his boxers. He had no idea Whitney was already up and preparing to leave until he opened his eyes to find her not lying next to him. His heart immediately skipped a beat at the thought of her being gone and him losing her for good.

Just as he was about to jump up and search for her, she came into the room. Dressed in only her robe, Whitney pretended as if he wasn't even there. Even though she'd used his shoulder to cry on the night before she still wasn't fuckin' wit him. Koran could kiss her ass. Whitney opened the doors to her walk-in closet and scanned the rack of clothes for something to wear.

"Where you going?" he asked, looking at the clock. It was only ten a.m.

"Should I wear my orange smock dress or a tank top and my 7 for All Mankind maternity jeans?" she spoke out loud to herself, disregarding his question.

"So after all that apologizing and shit I did and you crying, you still on that bullshit?" Koran barked.

"Yeah, I think I'ma wear the orange dress," she continued, taking it off the hanger.

"Where are you going?"

Whitney still wouldn't respond.

"A'ight, that's what's up." He got up, walked over to his dresser and began pulling out clothes, too.

"Muthafuckas love to play games. Well, guess what? I do, too."

"What are you doing?" Whitney finally spoke.

"Oh, now you wanna talk? I'll tell you about muthafuckas." Koran laughed. "You ain't hear me when I asked you where you was going, Whitney?"

"I don't have to tell you where I'm going."

"Well, guess what, ma? Wherever you go, I'ma go. When you look over yo' shoulder, expect to see me there."

"Koran, please, go sit down." She waved him off.

"Man, please, you got me fucked up."

"Whatever."

"Whatever," he repeated. "Let me tell yo' lil' ass something." He gripped her waist and pulled her close. "I ain't none of these lil' lame ass niggas you been fuckin' wit the last eight years, so don't ever in your life come out your neck at me sideways. If you got a problem, come holla at me so we can discuss it. Now I told you, I ain't fuckin' that bitch and I ain't been fuckin' that bitch! But if you wanna act all crazy and shit, I'ma act crazy right along wit yo' ass until you tell me what the fuck is wrong wit you!"

"I'M DYING!" she screamed so loud her neighbors could hear.

"What you mean you dying?" Koran released her and stepped back.

"I have leukemia." She inhaled deeply as tears rolled from the corners of her eyes.

"C'mon, Whitney, if you wanna break up then say it, but you ain't gotta say no ignorant shit like that."

"I'm not playing. I'm tellin' the truth."

"Yeah, okay, Whitney. You got leukemia. Tell me anything."

"Why the fuck would I lie to you about something like that?"

"Man, get the fuck outta here." He balled up his fists, pissed. "You ain't got no goddamn cancer! You just mad 'cause you ran into ole' girl and now you wanna run again! Well, guess what? If that's what you wanna do, then step! Go the fuck head 'cause I ain't got time for the games, ma! This shit here is too much." Koran threw his hands in the air. "Ya'll muthafuckas is gettin' on my nerves! First, I had to argue wit Trina! Now I got to turn around and argue wit yo' ass? Nah, I'm not having it! If you wanna run, run!"

"You know what? You's a selfish muthafucka! Everything always gotta be about you! Maybe Trina wasn't lying! Maybe ya'll are together, since you want me to go so bad!"

"A'ight, yeah, I'm wit her. Now what? What you want me to do? Buy you a plot?"

For a second it seemed as if time stood still. The little air Whitney had left in her lungs had been sucked away by Koran's words. She could visualize herself falling into a heap on the floor, but her legs were frozen stiff. Whitney had never felt so alone. How could the one person she depended on most hurt her so?

"Fuck you," she spat, slapping his face so hard she left her handprint.

Koran never saw the slap coming. He thought Whitney was just playing. There couldn't be any truth in her words. There just couldn't be, because, if there were, what did that mean for them? If Whitney had cancer that meant she would be leaving him once again. Why would God do that to him, to them?

"Whitney, come here," he begged, trying to grab her.

"Don't touch me." She spun around on her heels, causing him to jump back. "Fuck you! Yo' ass gots to go! I'm sick of this shit! This is the time in my life where I am supposed to be happy for once, but no, here I am five months pregnant with fuckin' leukemia! I thought I was done with this shit!"

"What you mean you thought you were done? What, you had cancer before?"

"Don't you get it?! I lied! That's why I left back in high school! My parents found a chemotherapy center in Chicago. That's why we moved. I didn't want anybody to see me sick. I didn't want anybody to see me throw up ten times a day or shit on myself. I didn't want anybody to see me so fatigued I couldn't even walk without help. I didn't want anybody to see me lose my fuckin' hair," Whitney screamed as she picked up a crystal vase and threw it.

"I can't even finish school now! But you know what makes it worse? I had to find out about your other bitch on the same day I learned I have cancer again! Do you know how that made me feel? I felt like just saying fuck it and dying right then and there! Hell, I should have, 'cause from the looks of things I'm gonna die, anyway!"

"Quit saying shit like that," Koran yelled. "You're not dying!"

"How you know? This is my second time getting cancer, Koran! You really think I'ma survive that shit twice? Picture that! Nothing ever happens the same way twice!"

"This is some bullshit." Koran plopped down onto the bed and covered his face with his hands. "You not gon' leave me again." He broke down and cried. "Fuck that! That shit ain't happening!"

"Koran, calm down," Whitney pleaded, wrapping her arms around him. She hated to see him defeated. "Don't do that. You gon' make it worse."

"How the fuck am I supposed to deal with this shit, Whitney?" He looked up at her with glossy eyes. "We just got back together."

"I don't know, baby. I wish I could tell you." She used her thumb to wipe his face. "You just have to."

"Man, I can't believe this. Here I am thinking everything is cool and here come this shit."

"The only thing we can do at this point is pray and be optimistic. I mean it's not like I'm gon' die tomorrow. At least I hope not," she joked, trying to make light of the situation.

"That shit ain't funny, man."

"I know it's not. I'm sorry."

"So that's just it. They can't do anything to help you?"

"Since I have acute leukemia my doctor wanted me to start chemo immediately. So I go in tomorrow to register at the David C. Pratt Cancer Center."

"What time you gotta be there?"

"I have to be there by nine, but that's just to register. Once I've registered I have to go back for my first treatment."

"And it's not going to hurt the baby?"

"No, just me, unfortunately."

"This shit here is too much. I swear to God it is."

"We can get through this though, babe. I know we can. I mean, I have to. I'm not trying to not see my baby grow up. But just in case things don't go as I plan, I do want to start doing all the things I've never done before." "Like what?" Koran wiped his face.

"Watch the sunrise, witness a miracle, get married." She giggled.

"Look at you." Koran laughed some too.

"I'm for real."

"You know anything you want to do, I'ma hold you down."

FINDING FOREVER

Nobody said a word. Total and utter silence filled the cold, sterile room as Whitney and Koran awaited the chemotherapy technologist's arrival. Today was the day they'd been dreading. Neither of them had been able to sleep the night before. Whitney lay in Koran's arms as both of their minds traveled to unwanted places. Now here they were facing their worst fears. Whitney inhaled and exhaled repeatedly, hoping that would slow down her heart rate.

She'd gone through the process of getting her blood pressure, height and weight taken. She'd even had an intravenous catheter inserted into her arm, but to go through her first chemotherapy treatment in six years would be the hardest part of all. It was like admitting that cancer had conquered her again and won.

And although she'd been here before in life, this time was different. She was no longer just living for herself. The baby girl growing inside her belly depended on her survival for its own. Whitney planned on doing anything and everything she could to ensure that her child made it into the world, even if that meant giving up her own life.

"How are you doing, Whitney?" The chemo tech, whose name was Cassandra, smiled and hugged her.

"As good as I can be, I guess." She forced herself to smile.

"Well, hopefully what we're about to do will make everything better. Your name is Koran, right? You're Whitney's boyfriend?"

"Yeah," Koran looked up and replied.

"How are you?"

"I'm good."

"Now we're going to give her medication after treatment, but there still may be some side effects."

"Like what?" Koran asked, concerned.

"Some of the side effects are pain, diarrhea, constipation, mouth sores, hair loss, nausea, and vomiting. So you just really have to be prepared to take care of her."

"A'ight." He nodded, taking it all in.

"Good. So Miss Whitney, are you ready?"

"Yeah, let's get started."

Whitney sat back in the recliner and got comfortable. Chemo treatments could last for several hours. Koran watched closely as Cassandra placed a needle into Whitney's arm and drugs began to drip into her veins. The sight of his five-month pregnant girlfriend receiving chemo crushed Koran's soul. To him, Whitney was as fragile as a Faberge Egg.

But what scared him the most was that she looked so at peace. Her eyes were closed. The white empire waist maternity dress and yellow cashmere cardigan she wore complimented her round belly perfectly. Whitney was the most beautiful women he'd ever seen. Every now and then the baby would kick, reminding him of the importance of the chemo working and Whitney getting better.

The thought of how he would raise a child without her by his side haunted his mind every second of the day. The fact that his being a single parent was a possibility fucked him up inside. Koran didn't understand why God would bring her back into his life just for things to be the way they were. They were supposed to ride off into the sunset and live happily ever after.

There was so much he had yet to share with her. They were supposed to explore the world together, hand in hand. Koran had always envisioned them getting married, having children and watching their grandchildren grow up. This whole cancer thing was fucking up his fantasy. Losing her for good wasn't a part of the equation.

Quietly, he took her hand. Whitney opened her eyes and revealed an angelic smile. On the outside she seemed so confident and brave. Koran wished he had an ounce of her courage. She was dealing with the situation better than he was and he wasn't even the one with cancer.

"You sure you're ready for all this?" she asked in a soft tone.

"No," Koran answered, afraid.

"You'll be okay." Whitney released his hand and rubbed his head.

"I hope so, baby. I hope so."

FINDING FOREVER

"How you feel?" Koran asked as he and Whitney pulled up to his house.

"I'm good, baby. Stop asking me that." She laughed.

"I'm just making sure."

"Well, yes, I'm fine."

"A'ight." He turned the engine off.

"And whose house are we at? It's beautiful."

"Mine . . . I mean ours."

"This is your place?" Whitney pointed her finger toward the house.

"Yeah."

"Do you realize that I have never been here?"

"I know. That's why I wanted to bring you. I got something I want to show you."

Koran hopped out and ran around the car to open Whitney's door. Holding his hand, she carefully stepped out. It was like she was in another land. Koran's house was breathtaking. It was like something she'd seen on HGTV. It was an Old Victorian row house, located on a quiet street in Lafayette Square.

"Koran, this is gorgeous. Oh my god," she gushed. "Why have you never brought me here before?"

"'Cause we spend so much time at your crib that I kinda forgot I had one of my own."

"How could you ever forget about something like this?" she wondered out loud as he opened the door.

Koran's living room was huge. It was more than twice the size of hers. Mahogany hardwood floors gave the space a warm, welcoming appeal, but the decor needed a woman's touch. The typically manly furnishings consisted of a leather sectional sofa, a cocktail table, flat screen television and an entertainment system.

"Your place is nice, baby."

"Our place," he corrected her.

"You really want me to move in here with you?"

"Yeah, I mean your place is cool, but we can't raise no baby there. You got concrete floors, ma. That ain't gon' work."

"You are right about that."

"And, plus, you only got one bedroom. Where the baby gon' sleep?"

"So much stuff has been going on that I hadn't really thought about that."

"Well, I have. My place has three bedrooms, so we more than good. You feel me?"

"I feel you."

"Now come upstairs wit me. I wanna show you something."

With her hand in his, Koran led Whitney up two flights of stairs. On the third floor of the house was his bedroom. He'd gone for a very minimalist look. There wasn't a lot of furniture in the space, but the little there was, was fly as hell. The first thing Whitney laid eyes on was his Asian-inspired platform bed, which was black with a red, sloped headboard. The comforter was a striking combination of black and red swirls over a white background.

A small off-white nightstand sat on one side of the bed and on top of it was a glass bowl filled with live goldfish. On the other side of the room was an off-white dresser with a lamp on it. The wall across from the bed held a huge flat screen television. But what topped the entire room off was that the roof of the bedroom was made completely of glass so you could see the sky.

"Now we can watch the sunrise every morning if you want to."

"Koran, oh my god, this is so sweet." She hugged his neck. "Has this always been like this or did you do it for me?"

"I did it for you." He kissed her lips passionately.

Whitney loved kissing Koran. His kisses were always so sweet and fulfilling. Whitney released her lips from his and replied, "Thank you, baby."

"You're welcome. Now come on. Let's find us something to eat, I'm starving."

FINDING FOREVER

It was an unusually windy August afternoon. A cool wind swept through the air. Koran stood on the porch with his hands in his pockets. Sheek had just pulled up in front of his house so they could talk. Normally they'd talk indoors, but the conversation he and Sheek were about to have couldn't be held indoors. Sheek stepped out his Mercedes Benz S600 Sedan, fresh to death in a fitted white v-neck T-shirt and army fatigue style baggy shorts. A pair of brand new, brown tweed high-top Chuck Taylors completed his look.

Sheek surveyed his surroundings, and then chirped the alarm. Even though he was in front of his homeboy's house he could never be too sure. Koran suppressed a laugh. Sheek was always overly cautious. Koran couldn't hate, though. Sheek's cautiousness was one of the characteristics he liked most about him. Slightly perturbed by what was so important, Sheek made his way up the steps.

"What up?" Koran raised his hand for five and a handshake.

"You, nigga." Sheek gave him a pound. "What the fuck was so important that you had to drag me out my house? My chick was just about to give me some ass."

"Watch yo' fuckin' mouth. I don't wanna hear that shit."

"Well, what the fuck is it then?"

"You know you my man, right?"

"Yeah." Sheek looked at him funny. "You ain't about to come out the closet or no shit like that, is you?"

"Sheek, don't make me slap the shit outta you."

"I'm just sayin', you actin' all serious and shit."

"Whateva. Look some shit about to change."

"Shit like what?"

"I'ma about to bow on out and hand everything to you. I already talked to Tony, my connect, and let him know that you gon' be handling things from now on."

"Where all this coming from? We doing good out here in the streets. You at the height of your run. Why the fuck you wanna give this shit up now?"

"'Cause man . . . I got a lotta shit I need to take care of." Koran turned his head and shuffled his feet.

"What's the deal? Holla at me. What the fuck could be more important than gettin' this money? I mean, don't get me wrong, I'm honored that you wanna turn shit over to ya' boy, but I'm just a little confused right now. We supposed to be in this shit together. Since we was lil' shorties on the block, we dreamed of gettin' where we are right now. So what the fuck has changed? I know you got yo' seed coming and all, but what that got to do with anything?"

"I feel you, but sellin' dope ain't all I wanna do with my life. And on top of that me and Whitney going through some deep shit right now."

"Talk to me."

"She sick," Koran responded with a solemn look on his face.

"Quit overexaggerating shit, Koran. Of course she gon' be sick, she's pregnant."

"Nah, man, she sick, sick. She got leukemia."

"You bullshittin'?" Sheek threw his head back in disbelief.

"Nah."

"Damn, that's fucked up." Sheek spoke slowly rubbing his chin. "You a'ight?"

"I'm good. She the one in pain and what fuck me up is that I can't do shit about it."

"Where she at now?"

"Upstairs sleep. She just started chemo about a month ago. We hoping she gon' be a'ight, but shit been hard man. I thought watching my mama gettin' high was something, but this shit right here ain't no joke. Almost every other day she sick, throwing up or having diarrhea."

"Damn," Sheek whispered in a daze.

"That's why I'm callin' it quits. And besides that, I'd rather get out now before I fall off or end up locked up. You can't stay on top forever, my nigga, remember that. I'm tryin' to get my shit in order. I gotta get this GED situation wrapped up and then after that I'ma enroll in school. Plus, since she's so sick I gotta get all the baby stuff and fix the room up."

"You know if you need my help I got you."

"Oh, I ain't even worried about that. I know you do," Koran confirmed with another handshake.

Inside the house, Whitney lay on her back in bed. Her once peaceful sleep had quickly turned into a dramatic struggle to wake up. She felt as if she was sinking into a bottomless pit and if she didn't wake up soon she never would. Fear overtook her body as her head tossed and turned. Whitney's mouth longed to scream for help, but the words wouldn't escape her lips. Her body was so tense that breathing became a chore.

There had to be a way out. If she fought harder she'd be released from the torturous cell her mind had put her in. There was no way she was gonna let her illness or bad dreams win. Forcing herself to wake up, Whitney jumped out of sleep in a hot sweat. Her eyes did a quick assessment of the room to ensure that she was still alive and not in heaven. London started licking her arm, confirming her whereabouts.

After ruffling his fur, she called out for Koran, who, before she fell asleep, had been by her side. He was no longer there. Whitney held her stomach and carefully got out of bed. The cold hardwood floor felt like icicles prickling her feet as she made her way to the master bathroom. Using her index finger, she flicked on the light.

The reflection gazing back at her in the mirror alarmed Whitney. She looked like a sick person. There was no color in her skin, dark circles surrounded her eyes, and her lips were chapped and dry. She was no longer the stunning beauty she once was. Whitney often wondered if Koran even found her attractive anymore. If she was him she wouldn't.

He had to be overwhelmed and tired of cleaning up behind her and feeding her. There was only so much a person his age could take. Whitney expected him to walk out and leave her any day now. Disgruntled by her appearance, she hurriedly washed her face.

"Baby," Koran called out as he entered the bedroom. "Where you at?"

"In the bathroom," she yelled back, drying her face with a cotton towel.

"You okay?"

"Yeah, why you ask me that?" she lied, flicking off the bathroom light.

"'Cause." Koran looked at her and then at the bed.

Whitney's eyes followed his to the bed, where a clump of black hair sat on her pillow.

"Well, I didn't think that would be happening so soon."

"You a'ight?" Koran asked, concerned.

"I'm fine." Whitney twisted up her face as if she didn't care. "As a matter of fact, let me show you how fine I am." She turned around and went back into the bathroom.

Uncertain of what she was about to do, Koran followed her. Whitney opened the cabinet underneath the sink and pulled out a pair of clippers Koran stored there.

"What you about to do with that?"

"What does it look like I'm about to do? I'm about to take care of this shit right now." She plugged the cord into the socket.

Once the clippers were plugged up, Whitney turned them on and proceeded to shave the right side of her head. Fuck, if she was going to be a victim she was gonna face her illness head on. She'd been here before so there was nothing to fear. It was just hair. If she lived long enough it would grow back someday. Koran was once again astounded by her courage. So much so that before Whitney could shave the other side of her head, he took the clippers from her hand.

"C'mon, Koran, stop. Give them back. I know what I'm doing." She reached for them.

"I know that, but I want to do it, too."

Whitney's heart melted. "Koran, you don't have to do that."

"I know I don't. I want to." He looked deep into her eyes to assure her.

No doubt entered his mind as he too shaved the right side of his head, eliminating his locs. It didn't matter that it had taken four years for his hair to grow to the length it was. Cutting his locs was the least he could do to show Whitney how much he loved her and stood by her side. He was in this for the long haul.

Whitney's not having any hair wasn't going to drive him away. If anything, the two of them shaving their heads together brought them closer together. Almost an hour later, Koran and Whitney stood peering into the mirror admiring their new reflections. Whitney was still a knock out. Her dimples seemed to glow even brighter now that she didn't have any hair to hide behind.

"I kinda like you wit no hair, ma." He kissed the back of her head.

"You don't look too bad yourself." She smiled. "How long you plan on keeping this look?"

"As long as you keep yours."

"So me, you and the baby gon' be walking around here lookin' like triplets?" Whitney joked.

"Looks like it."

Koran paused briefly before looking in the mirror and speaking again. He and Whitney were a perfect match. No other woman would look better by his side. Koran massaged her belly, then closed his eyes and kissed her neck.

"Marry me?" he asked with his head resting on her shoulder.

"What?" Whitney stared into the mirror at him, taken aback.

"You heard me. Let's get married."

"When?"

"Before the baby is born."

"Are you sure?" She turned around to face him.

"Yeah." He held her in a warm embrace. "So what you say?"

"Yes."

CHAPTER EIGHT

You and I Till the Day We Die

It'd been a while since Koran pulled into the driveway in front of the house he used to call home. The last time he'd set foot on the property was when he and Trina got into it and he'd pulled out his gun. After that night Koran made a vow to himself never to let Trina take him to that level of being pissed off again. It wasn't good for anybody, especially Malik. He didn't have the energy to fight, anyway. For the past month and a half his life had been emotionally draining enough.

Watching the person he loved most in life deteriorate right before his very own brown eyes ate away at him day in and day out. With each passing day, the fact that Whitney might die became more evident. Death loomed over her like a black plague. It was almost as if he could see it in her eyes. She wasn't her usual perky self. Her energy level was at an all-time low. She couldn't even take a step without him being there to hold her hand. Koran couldn't fathom the mental anguish Whitney had to be going through day after day.

Knowing that at any moment the breath you took could be your last was a muthafucka. Koran hated to leave her side. It scared him for her to be out of his sight. Every time he had to leave thoughts filled his mind that today might be the day they had to go their separate ways. But then he'd think back on all the things they had yet to do.

Whitney still had to approve the shade of pink she wanted the baby's nursery to be painted and neither of them had decided on a name. Whitney liked Kimora and Koran liked Harlow. The crib had to be assembled and on top of that, Koran still had to study for his online GED course. Things would be better in due time, he continued to tell himself.

Koran reluctantly opened the driver's side door and got out. Raindrops fell at a slow pace from the sky, landing on his brown leather bomber jacket. He tilted his brown Yankees cap to the left and made his way to the door. He loathed the fact that he had to deal with Trina in order to see Malik. She was gonna do everything in her power to start a fight. Koran wasn't in the mood for it, so his visit with Malik would most definitely end up being a short one.

Everything in him wanted to bust Trina in her mouth for lying to Whitney, but hitting her wouldn't even be worth it. Trina was still gonna be sad and miserable at the end of the day. Instead of using his key, Koran rang the doorbell and three rings later, Trina finally came to the door. Koran knew she was on some ignorant shit, but he decided to let it go for Malik's sake.

"What you want?" she shot at him with an attitude.

"Malik upstairs?" Koran looked the other way and ignored her.

"No."

"What you mean, no?"

"Like I said, he ain't here, and frankly I don't even understand why yo' ass is here. I told you to step a while ago. What, you ain't got the hint?"

"You know what, Trina?" A light bulb went off in his head. "You right. What the fuck am I stressing for? Malik ain't even my son, so I'ma do like you said and step. Tell Malik to holla at me when he turns eighteen."

"What does that mean?"

"I'm done." Koran turned his back to her and walked to his car.

He'd missed his son terribly, but dealing with Trina and her nasty attitude was too much for him. All the back and forth, arguing and fighting, wasn't necessary. He could show her better than he could tell her.

Trina held the door open with a surprised expression on her face. This time she'd gone too far. She had never meant for Koran to get so upset that he'd throw in the towel. Once again she'd let her own selfish needs get in the way of the happiness of her son. How would she explain to Malik that she'd driven the only father figure he'd known away? She couldn't and there was no way on God's green earth she would.

FINDING FOREVER

The day Whitney had dreamed of for the past eight years was finally here. September 6, 2008 was the day she would become Koran McKnight's wife. Things couldn't be better. For the first time in weeks she didn't feel sick. Her skin wasn't as golden as it once was, but that was nothing a little makeup and body bronzer couldn't fix. Her parents, Joan and Oscar, were in town and in their own separate room getting dressed. Koran was at the wedding site. The last time they'd spoken; the wedding planner, decorators, caterers and reverend had arrived.

Everything was going just like she'd dreamed. Her prince charming was about to make her the happiest woman on earth. Nothing compared to the way he made her feel inside. Without him she didn't know where she'd be. He lifted her heart and spirits with just one smile. With him she felt like she could reach the highest mountaintop.

Angels sang in her ear every time she said his name. There wasn't any doubt in her mind that their love wouldn't stand the test of time. And, yes, in the past she'd dated other men, but Whitney had never felt a love like the one she and Koran shared.

After putting the finishing touches on her makeup, Whitney

sat back and took a good look at herself in the mirror. The reflection gazing back at her was stunning. She couldn't wait to see the look on Koran's face when he laid eyes on her.

"You ready, sweetheart?" her mother asked, peeking her head inside the door.

"I was born ready," Whitney replied, standing up.

Fifteen minutes later, they arrived at the wedding site in a stretch limousine. Nervous jitters filled the bottom of Whitney's stomach as the driver opened the door. The baby was kicking. Whitney took a calming breath and realized that she had nothing to worry about. This was her destiny. The elevator ride to the rooftop of the building was short.

Once the wedding planner gave the cue, her parents began their walk down the aisle. When Whitney heard Chrisette Michelle's soulful voice singing, she knew it was her time to go. This was the moment she'd been waiting for. Her eyes immediately filled with tears when she and Koran's eyes connected. Every fantasy she had ever wished for had come true.

A huge white gazebo, draped with white sheer curtains that were held open by iceberg garden roses and greenery, overlooked the city's skyline. Twinkling lights surrounded the gazebo and bordered the rooftop. Two medium-size Grecian columns filled with white roses, nerine lilies and gardenia foliage sat on both sides of the rose petal covered aisle leading to her king.

Koran was the very definition of what a man was. Not only was he caring and hardworking, but he was fine as hell. The suit he wore fit his measurements to a tee. It was black, but the button-up shirt he wore underneath it was white. The satin tie he wore around his neck was white, as well. The smooth, spinning waves in his hair were dizzying. Whitney swore she could smell his Yves Saint Laurent Cologne at the other end of the aisle where she stood.

A bright smile lit up his face. Words couldn't describe how undeniably beautiful Whitney was. Some of her hair had grown back, so she rocked a sleek, short cut. Her makeup was exquisite—grey, smoky eye shadow, pink blush and almost nude, pink lip-gloss. Diamond chandelier earrings swung from her ears, enhancing her features. The dress she wore highlighted her baby bump. She had chosen a white, strapless, empire-waist gown that swept the floor, with a trail of rosettes stretching from her right breast to the back of the dress.

Only four people were in attendance so Koran and Whitney opted not to have any groomsmen or bridesmaids. Whitney gave a warm smile to her parents, Sheek and Malik, as she made her way down the aisle. The sun had just begun to set. An orange and gold hue painted the sky. After handing her mother her bouquet, Whitney and Koran stood face-to-face, holding hands.

"We are in this holy and sacred hour to witness the uniting of these two devoted hearts. This most blessed and lasting human relationship was first celebrated with quiet vows in a time of man's sins. God saw that it was not good for man to live alone, so he created a woman and gave her onto him for his companion, his wife. Who then in the name of the Heavenly Father gives this woman to marry?" Reverend Joseph asked.

"I do," Whitney's father spoke up.

"Marriage can be a lifelong unfolding of love and kindness, backed by the will to make it last. Koran, you are now entering into a relationship that may be met with plenty privileges, but also many obligations. This woman you love is about to become your wife. Your joy will be her joy. Your sorrow will be her sorrow. Your people will be her people and your God, her God."

After a brief pause Reverend Joseph turned to Whitney.

"Whitney, you too, are entering into a relationship with many privileges, but also many obligations. The man you love is about to become your husband. Your love will be his inspiration and your prayers his tower of strength."

Reverend Joseph faced Koran and said, "Do you, Koran, take this woman to be your lawfully wedded wife, to love and respect her, honor and cherish her, through health and sickness, prosperity and adversity, so long as you both shall live?"

"I do," Koran answered with tears in his eyes.

"Do you, Whitney, take this man to be your lawfully wedded husband, to love and respect him, honor and cherish him, through health and sickness, prosperity and adversity, so long as you both shall live?"

"I do," she sobbed, barely able to speak.

"May these rings be blessed as a symbol of this affectionate union. May you find in one another the love for which all men and women yearn. May you grow in understanding and compassion. May the home you establish together be such a place of sanctuary that all who are here today and others find that these two are true friends. Koran, you may now recite the vows you have written for Whitney."

"Whitney, from the first day I laid eyes on you I loved you. I knew you would one day become my wife. Your beauty is what attracted me to you in the beginning, but I see now that your beauty is more than skin deep. You've come back into my life and changed it for the better. Everything I do now makes sense. You've given me permission to be who I am and as a result of that, I'm willing to share all I have and am with you. I don't know how I ever got by without you. Every night I thank God that I found you. I love you, ma."

"Whitney." Minister Joseph nodded his head toward her to let her know it was her turn to speak.

"It's not so easy loving me. It gets so complicated, all the things you got to be. Everything's changing, but you're the truth. Nothing or no one can replace the love I have for you. Right by your side is where I belong. You're all I know. I don't feel safe in this world without you. I pray that we're never apart. My dreams have come true, because of you. You're the reason I believe in love. There is no low or high of my heart you haven't seen. And don't ask me why I love you, because it's obvious. Your tenderness has made me a better woman. I love you from now until the end of time."

"Koran, when you place this ring on Whitney's hand, please repeat after me."

Koran gently took Whitney's left hand.

"With this ring . . ."

"With this ring," Koran followed.

"I thee wed."

"I thee wed," he spoke, sliding a three-carat canary yellow diamond ring onto her finger. "With my worldly goods, I thee endow. In sickness and in health, in poverty or in wealth, for better or for worse, till death do us part."

"Whitney, when you place this ring on Koran's hand, please repeat after me."

"With this ring . . .

"With this ring," she said as her bottom lip trembled.

"I thee wed."

"I thee wed. With my worldly goods, I thee endow. In sickness and in health, in poverty or in wealth, for better or for worse, till death do us part."

Heavy tears dripped down her face and onto her chin.

"Koran and Whitney, your families are here to bless your marriage. Your family and friends have all been a part of your individual lives and have shared with you your hopes and your dreams . . . your triumphs . . . your sorrows . . . your suffering. Now that you have pledged your love for each other and have sealed your pledge with marriage, I do by the power vested in me pronounce you husband and wife. You may now kiss your bride."

This was the moment Koran had been waiting for. The love of his life was now, finally, his wife. Koran stepped forward and cupped Whitney's face in his hands. Time seemed to stand still as he gazed into her eyes. Without warning, he placed his lips onto hers. Whitney melted in ecstasy as the white butterflies they'd ordered were released into the air. Koran's caramel kisses devoured her and locked up in his embrace, where she belonged. This was love in its truest, rarest form. Whitney prayed to the heavens that the feeling she was feeling would last forever.

FINDING FOREVER

The sky was darker than usual as Koran stepped outside. It was a stark shade of gray. The leaves on the trees were fading fast and a dewy mist saturated the ground. Something in the atmosphere alarmed Koran's soul. He didn't know what it was, but it had him on edge. The entire morning his stomach had been doing flip-flops. Koran tried his best to shake the unsettling feeling as he made his way down the walkway and to the mailbox. Advertisements and other miscellaneous mail filled the box. Koran was about to dump all of it in the trash, but then he came across a letter from Jefferson City, MO. His GED test results were back.

A crisp, cold air swept through Koran's fingers as he eagerly tore open the envelope. A feeling of accomplishment overtook him as he realized he'd passed with flying colors. Whitney was the first person on his list that he wanted to share his news with. Closing the mailbox, he ran up the walkway and into the house.

Whitney was upstairs lying down. Since the wedding she'd become even more fatigued and weak. Her body had completely stopped reacting to chemotherapy. With each visit the doctors felt less and less hopeful that she'd survive, but Whitney stayed positive. She was a fighter. She'd beat cancer before, so no one could tell her she couldn't beat it again. Back upstairs, Koran entered the bedroom to find her sitting up with a pillow behind her back, propping her up.

The little hair that had grown back was long gone. Whitney was so embarrassed by her appearance she refused to walk around without a scarf on her head. Dressed in a paisley pink silk scarf, a pink spaghetti strap camisole, pajama bottoms and socks, Whitney gave Koran a half smile. He couldn't see it though. A hospital mask covered her face. Whitney was in so much pain that even smiling hurt.

"Babe," he said, excited. "Guess what? I got good news." He took a seat on the edge of the bed near Whitney's feet.

"What is it, baby?" she whispered back. Even her voice sounded weak.

"I took my GED test and I passed. I got the results back today." Koran held up the test results.

"Congratulations, baby. Why didn't you tell me you were studying for it?"

"'Cause I wanted to surprise you."

"I'm so happy for you." She stretched out her arms for a hug and Koran quickly took her into his arms.

"I love you, baby. I'm so proud of you." She kissed his cheek.

"Thanks, ma."

"So what's next?"

"Since the school year has already started, I'ma register for classes in December so I can start in January."

"That's what's up. I'ma have me a college man," Whitney joked.

"Oh, I ain't stopping there. Remember those vacant buildings on the Rock Road in Wellston?" Whitney nodded her head. "I've been thinkin' about buying them."

"I think that's a great idea."

"Yeah, I'ma talk to some people about that soon."

"Can you help me to the bathroom, baby? I have to use it."

"You know I got you." Koran held her hand and helped her up.

Suddenly, Whitney started to feel faint. The walls were closing in on her and the bathroom seemed so far away. It was like she was walking down a never-ending corridor that led to nowhere. Her legs felt like Jell-O. Whitney couldn't feel anything, because all of her senses were rapidly shutting down.

Koran was right next to her, holding her arm, but he was none the wiser. Whitney wanted to warn him, but the words wouldn't form. Before he knew it, her body had gone limp. Whitney almost fell face forward on the floor, but Koran wouldn't allow it. His quick reflexes kicked into high gear and instead of falling forward, she fell to her knees.

Koran gently laid her on her back, and then raced over to the phone. His heart raced a mile a minute as he dialed. It seemed like his fingers weren't moving fast enough. Then the phone began to ring. A second later, an operator came on the line.

"911, what's your emergency?"

"My wife is pregnant and she has cancer. She just passed out. I

NEED HELP NOW! I THINK SHE'S DYING!!!!!!!"

FINDING FOREVER

Life continued to go on around Koran. Nurses did their rounds, janitors cleaned, and visitors got snacks from the vending machines. But Koran was stuck in time. His mind wouldn't stop going back to the moment Whitney fainted. Why hadn't he noticed that she was in distress? Koran had trained himself to be prepared for such a situation. He had promised to always protect her and he'd failed.

The look on her face before she fainted flashed before his eyes. Whitney lay unconscious for only a matter of minutes, but it had felt like an eternity. Koran called out her name over and over, and she hadn't replied. After gently shaking her, she came to.

"Baby . . . what happened?" she asked.

"You passed out, ma. The paramedics are on their way," Koran assured her, kissing her face repeatedly.

An hour had passed and Koran now sat alone in the dreary waiting room, dying for answers. Whitney's parents were on their way, but it would take them another three hours to get there from Chicago. Koran was a wreck. Moral support needed to come soon before he lost his mind and spazzed out on everybody in the hospital.

"Mr. Mcknight," a voice said from behind him.

"Yes?" Koran spun around in his seat, and then stood up.

"I'm Dr. Rohan."

"Nice to meet you." Koran shook his hand. "How is my wife doing? Is she okay?"

"She's doing okay for now, but it doesn't look good. I've looked over her file and I saw that she is no longer responding to chemo. So at this point there is really nothing else we can do. I know this may be difficult to hear, but I expect that Whitney only has a couple more weeks to live, if that."

Koran swallowed hard. He was speechless. His heart had dropped to his knees.

"Now, because of this," Dr. Rohan continued, "and the fact that your wife is only seven months pregnant, we're going to have to take the baby by performing an emergency C-Section."

"When?"

"Today. In an hour or so. Dr. Chancellor is prepping her right now."

"Does my wife know this?"

"Yes, we've already informed her."

"Can I go in and see her now?"

"Yes, she's been asking for you. She's in room 202."

Shaken by the news, Koran slowly made his way into Whitney's room. The scene was like something straight out of an episode of ER. She lay in a motorized bed with IVs stuck in her arm and tubes stuck up her nose. A million machines were going at once, all to prolong her existence. One brown leather chair sat off to the side. The sound of the baby's heartbeat echoed through the air, crushing Koran's heart. He didn't know if he could go on without breaking down.

"Took you long enough," Whitney teased as he sat by her side.

"They just now let me come back. How you feelin'?" He took her hand.

"Great." She coughed. "For a dying woman."

"What I tell you about saying stuff like that?"

"I'm sorry, that was bad. How are you?"

"Don't worry about me. My only concern is you. I'ma be good."

"I know you are. That's why I don't have anything to worry about. Baby, you have far exceeded my expectations. You're gonna be a great father. I just know it."

"And you're going to be an even greater mom."

"No, I'm not." Whitney shook her head.

"Yes, you are," Koran protested.

"Koran, no I'm not. I'm dying, baby. I can feel it," she cried. "I'm going on, but I promise I'll be waiting for you."

"Stop saying shit like that. You not leaving me." Koran's bottom lip trembled as tears poured from his eyes.

The aching pain in his chest was unbearable. He wanted to shout and throw shit around. Koran had never been so upset in his life. No matter what he did, his life always turned to shit and Koran blamed God. He was the mastermind behind this whole thing. He knew how much Koran needed Whitney, but he planned on taking her away, anyway. What kind of God would do that to a person?

"Baby, listen, I need you to be strong, if not for me or yourself, then for the baby. She's gonna need you more than I ever did. And I know what you're thinking and it's not right. You can't be upset with God, Koran. I'm not. I've figured it all out. God had a bigger plan for me than what I had for myself. He sent you back to me for a reason and that was so I could finish my life . . . this life . . . here on earth . . . with you."

"But how am I supposed to deal with this shit, man?" Koran threw his head back in frustration and wiped snot from his nose.

"You'll figure out a way. The baby will keep you busy enough."

"I can't do this shit, man."

"Yes, you can and you will," Whitney reassured him, sliding her hand down his face.

"I guess, man." He shook his head, pissed.

"Excuse me." A nurse entered the room. "Sorry to interrupt. I'm Nurse Jackie." She extended her hand for a shake.

"How are you?" Koran shook her hand.

"Good, I'm here to check Whitney's and the baby's vital signs."

"No problem. I'ma be outside, a'ight?" He kissed the palm of Whitney's hand.

"Okay."

"You love me?"

"More than you'll ever know."

The door to Whitney's room closed quietly behind Koran as he made his way to the elevator. A zillion thoughts swam through his mind. Koran wanted terribly for this to all be a bad dream. The only problem was, the longer he lived in it the more things became clear that it wasn't. Koran was in desperate need of an herbal pick-me-up. He didn't want to think or feel anymore. He remembered he had an ounce of fresh purple haze and a brand new pack of cigarillo's stashed in his glove compartment. Just as the elevator doors opened and he was about to get on, Whitney's parents were getting off.

"Koran," Whitney's mother, Joan, exclaimed, running into his arms.

"How did ya'll get here so fast?" he asked shocked.

"We took a red eye. Where is Whitney? How is she doing?"

Koran pulled his in-laws to the side and gave them all the information he had. Whitney's parents were devastated, especially Whitney's father. When she was first diagnosed with leukemia he'd tried his best to shield his daughter from pain. She was his only child and baby girl. No matter the cost, he was going to save her. Oscar had used his savings and retirement fund so she could have the best treatment known to man and in the end it only worked for a while. Whitney had been cancer-free for almost six years. But this time he wouldn't be able to save her. There was nothing anyone could do and accepting that was killing him softly inside.

"Oscar, everything's going to be okay. We knew this was something that might happen," Joan consoled him. "We all have to be strong for Whitney and the baby. They're gonna need us, so we all have to band together for them."

"You're right, baby." Oscar wiped a tear from his eye, and then kissed her check.

"Koran, can I talk to you for a second?" Joan stepped off to the side.

"Yes, ma'am?"

"I just wanted you to know," she said, placing both of her hands on his arms. "That me and Mr. Ellis are here for you. If there is anything you need from us, just let us know."

"Okay."

"I've heard nothing but good things about you, so I know you are going to give this baby everything she needs. Whitney has complete faith in you and so do I."

"Thanks, I'ma do my best." Koran tried to convince himself.

"I know you are, sweetheart."

"Excuse me, Mr. McKnight," Nurse Jackie called. "I need you to follow me."

"I'll be right back," he told Joan. "What's going on?" he questioned as he and the nurse walked down the hall at a fast pace.

"We need you to get scrubbed up and ready, because we're getting ready to perform the C-Section now."

"Why? I thought the doctor said in an hour."

"We have to do it now, because the baby's heart rate is dropping."

Finding Forever

Ten minutes later, Koran, dressed in light blue scrubs, sat by Whitney's side as Dr. Chancellor prepared to make his first incision. Whitney lay flat on her back, with a light blue shower cap on her head. A light blue curtain prevented her from seeing what the doctor and nurses were doing. Beeping and buzzing noises filled the room. Whitney's entire body was numb. She couldn't even feel Koran holding her hand. He watched intently as the doctor used a small a knife to cut across the bottom of her abdomen.

"Whitney, would you like some music?" Nurse Jackie asked.

"No, I'm fine."

"Koran, you know you can stand up," the nurse announced.

"Oh." He shot up, nervous.

"As long as you don't pass out," she joked, trying to lift the somber mood. "Just let me know if you're gonna be queasy. We have a vomit bag right behind you."

"A'ight." He laughed some.

"Okay, Whitney, you're gonna feel a lot of pressure."

"Okay." She nodded, feeling it.

"You're doing great, ma." Koran kissed her forehead.

"I'm scared, baby." Whitney finally let her emotions show as tears dripped from her eyes.

"No, you're not. Remember, you're a big girl." He convinced himself to smile. "The baby's gonna be fine and so are you."

"Whitney," Dr. Chancellor said. "We have a big ole water bag we're gonna pop here in a second. I see some nice clear fluid and a head full of hair."

Once the entering of the peritoneal cavity and separation of the uterovesical fluid was completed, Dr. Chancellor placed his hand inside Whitney's abdomen and proceeded to pull the baby out. Nurse Jackie pressed down at the top of Whitney's abdomen so the baby would move forward, toward the doctor's hands.

"This baby's little! She's coming, she's coming! Ohhhhh, she's a beauty. We've got her chest out." The doctor continued to pull.

"She has jet black hair, just like you, ma." Koran smiled, happy, as the baby came all the way out.

"Ahhhhh, she's gorgeous!" Nurse Jackie chimed in. "Hi, sweetheart. What time is it?" she asked her assistant.

"Five-twenty-five p.m."

The shrill sounds of the baby crying overtook any other sounds being made. The nurses quickly wiped her off. Koran got his first up-close look at her when he cut the umbilical cord. She only weighed four pounds, but aside from her mother, she was the most exquisite creature he'd ever seen. Her skin was a rare shade of bamboo, and thick wavy black hair covered her head.

Almond shaped brown eyes, a Bambi nose and plump lips made up the rest of her facial features. She was just as had Koran envisioned she would be.

"What are you going to name her?" Dr. Chancellor asked as he closed Whitney's incision.

"Harlow," Whitney answered without even setting eyes on her baby yet.

"You sure?" Koran said from across the room.

"Yeah."

A few seconds later, Koran, along with Nurse Jackie, placed Harlow in an incubator and wheeled her over to Whitney. A tiny pink hat rested on her head. Like her mother, Harlow was bombarded with needles and plugs. The sight of her daughter brought satisfied tears to Whitney's eyes. She was everything she'd hoped for and more. Her little pink lips formed into a perfect pout.

"Can I touch her?" Whitney asked.

"Sure, you can," Nurse Jackie replied.

Two holes were on each side the incubator. Whitney stuck her hand inside the one closest to Harlow's hand. Her fingers were so small that one of Whitney's could touch all five of hers at the same time.

"Hi, baby, it's Mommy."

Harlow was sound asleep, but the sound of her mother's voice brought an instant smile to her face.

"I love you sooooo much," Whitney cried. Her face was soaked with tears.

"We're gonna have to take her now," Nurse Jackie explained.

"Alright." Whitney nodded, waving goodbye. "Take good care

of my baby."

"I will."

"I'm almost done, Whitney," Dr. Chancellor announced. "I want you to be able to spend as much time with your baby girl as possible."

"Are my parents here?" she questioned Koran.

"Yeah, they're out in the waiting room. I'ma go tell them what's up in a second. Are you okay?" Koran said with a concerned expression on his face. Whitney's lips had begun to turn blue and her fingertips were ice cold.

"I'm tired, baby." She struggled to keep her eyes open.

Whitney felt worn and feeble. She'd given all she had just to get to this point. Seeing her daughter come into the world was the last thing she'd prayed to God for. There was no more to be said or done and her body didn't have any more will to fight. She hated to give up and leave her family behind, but God's will had to be done.

It was her time to journey off into the sun, to a place that was nice and warm. She wasn't fearful, timid or afraid. Heaven's gates were welcoming her into their sanctuary with open arms. Whitney could hear Koran's voice off in the distance, calling her name, but it was too late.

"What's wrong with her?" he shouted.

"She's going into cardiac arrest," Dr. Chancellor replied. "You're going to have to leave the room, sir."

"No, I promised I'd stay by her side!"

"Sir, please step outside the room." Nurse Jackie pushed Koran back.

Two huge doors closed before Koran's face. A sense of complete and utter helplessness consumed him. Then the deafening sound of death rang in the air.

"BEEEEEEEEEEEEEEEEEEEEEEEEEEEEEEEEEEEEEEEEEEE EP!!!!!!!!"

CHAPTER NINE

5 Years Later

The sun shined brighter than ever and the trees swayed to a beat all their own. It was a glorious September morning. Birds chirped and squirrels ran along the sidewalk in search of something to eat. On the radio, Rickey Smiley, Ebony, and Gary with Da Tea joked about current events. While driving down the highway, Koran reflected on the past five years of his life. A lot had changed.

He'd gone to college and graduated with a Bachelor's degree in Business Administration. For the past year he'd been studying for his Master's. With the help of Whitney's parents and outside associates, he'd opened a cancer center called 'Hopes.' Since opening, they'd been able to successfully treat well over fifteen patients.

Trina had moved onto the next big baller, but they were able to get along without constantly beefing. Malik was now a teenager and playing football.

The biggest change in his life was Harlow. She was the apple of her daddy's eye. Koran had never known a love like the one they shared. Whitney was right. She kept him so busy he had no time to question whether or not he could he raise her without Whitney. There were times when he looked into Harlow's eyes and cried, and some nights were so dreadful he couldn't sleep. He missed the security of knowing Whitney would be there when he lay his head down at night. His lips longed for the taste of her mouth on his.

Nightmares of her death had plagued his dreams for months, but with time Koran's soul began to heal.

He couldn't mope around or be mad. Besides, his little girl needed him and he needed her. Now here they were, father and daughter, exploring a new adventure together. Koran nervously made his way into the parking lot of Harlow's school. Today was the first day of the school year and Harlow's first day of kindergarten. Koran, with his camcorder in hand, got out and opened the passenger side door. His leading lady was ready for her close-up.

"Are you sure I look good, Daddy?" Harlow asked before stepping out of the car.

Just like her mother, Harlow loved clothes. That day she wore an outfit her grandma Joan had picked out—a green pea coat inspired jacket with a white ruffled shirt underneath. The rest of the outfit consisted of a black skirt with matching suspenders, white and black polka dot tights and shiny patent leather Mary Janes. Harlow's long, curly hair was parted down the middle and twisted into spiral shaped pigtails and a little bit of baby hair graced her forehead. To complete her ensemble, she rocked a green purse and book bag.

"You look perfect, baby girl," Koran guaranteed, videotaping her.

"I can't be lookin' a mess, Daddy," she explained, getting out.

"You're not." Koran chuckled as they made their way into the building.

"Are you excited about your first day of kindergarten?" he asked.

"Uh-huh."

"Whose gonna pick you from school today?"

"You, Daddy." Harlow giggled as she stood in front of her classroom door.

"So what are you gonna learn today?"

"Ummm." She twisted from side to side. "Letteeeeeeeeers—"

"Letters and numbers," Koran joined in. "Are you gonna color?"

"Yep."

"What's your teacher's name?"

"Miss Welllllls."

"Miss Wells, wow. You know what?"

"What, Daddy?" Harlow laughed again.

"You remind me of someone special I used to know. She was smart and pretty and funny, just like you. And guess what?"

"What?"

"You look just like her, too. You even have the same dimples she had. Can you guess who I'm talkin' about?"

"Uh-huh."

"Who?"

"Mommy!"

"That's right, sweetheart." Koran reached out and hugged her with his free arm. "Now have a good day. I love you."

"I love you too, Daddy."

Koran turned off the camera and made his way back to the car. Outside, he took a look up at the sky and wondered if Whitney was watching. His question was answered when a white butterfly fluttered by. Koran couldn't help but smile. Although she wasn't physically there, Koran could feel her spirit. Their love had no limits. It was unique and one-of-a-kind. Whitney had shown him the light. His heart's dictionary defined her. There was no need for him to search for forever anymore, 'cause he'd already found it in her.

THESE BOOKS ARE AVAILABLE IN PAPERBACK AT
BOOKSTORES EVERYWHERE.

THEY CAN ALSO BE PURCHASED DIRECTLY FROM THE
PUBLISHER AT

WWW.PRIORITYBOOKS.COM

D E A T H
NO EXCEPTIONS!

It was one thing for William Earl Holly, an ex-con four months fresh out of State prison, broke and hungry for a quick major come up, to strong arm rob Queen City dope girl on the low - Monica Sparks, taking her coke, cash, and chromed out 190 Benz. But it was altogether something different when William put his hands on her child in the process. In the eyes of Monica and her thugged-out associates it was a fatal mistake. One in which they all were determined to have William answer for. But first, William had to be found. Follow Monica as she demonstrates in no uncertain terms what being motivated by an unhealthy emotion called REVENGE can do to a mutha.

ISBN 13: 978-0-9816483-6-1
ISBN 10: 0-9816483-6-3
http://www.myspace.com/karemtomblin
$14.95

Coming September 15, 2008.
Kareem is incarcerated in South Carolina.

Sex on the 2nd Floor
Or anywhere else you can get it!

Jessica Williamson never dreamed that the fire in her would unleash an insurmountable passion when she hired the sexy and handsome Travis Ingram to maintain the company's computer system. Not only did he capture her heart but his mere presence caused havoc, backstabbing, confusion and sexual tension at the office. Jessica finds herself changing from upstanding and happily married to an oversexed, overheated, and hot between the legs adulteress. Will Jessica and Travis control the passion that threatens to destroy everything they worked so hard to obtain? Or will they succumb to the passion in their hearts? Jazz Catrell weaves an interesting tale of love in the workplace and how listening to your heart is not always the right thing to do.

Distributors: Ingram, Baker and Taylor & Lushena
Amazon.com, Barnes & Noble.com
www.sex-on-the-second-floor.blogspaot.com

Email: jazzcatrell@yahoo.com
ISBN: 978-0-9753634-8-5
$14.95

Still Ghetto
The Sequel
Newest Release

Mary L. Wilson, Queen of the Ink Pen, returns with the highly anticipated sequel to Ghetto Luv. Join Mya and Libra once again as they battle against deception, destruction and death in the drama-filled streets of the Lou. Brazen and bold, the mistress of seduction is back and she is sexier than ever. With a major record deal, a handsome husband and a precious son, life couldn't be any better. But problems and trouble lingers near. The twists and turns that occur in this tangled tale will leave readers begging for more.

Mary L. Wilson
Queen of the Ink Pen
P.O. Box 150524
St. Louis, MO 63115
314-450-6634

Ghetto Luv
Urban novel takes you straight to the 'hood and leaves you laughing

Sassy. Urban. Funny. Mary Wilson's *Ghetto Luv* is "in your face," with the cat-and-mouse game between the Keke and Libra as the backdrop. Keke is one of the most handsome brothas in the 'hood, definitely smooth when it comes to the ladies.

Neighborhood diva Libra is described as "every man's dream and every woman's nightmare." She and her two girls rule the streets, but Libra is clearly the standout of the three. She is full of spunk, confidence and street smarts - the mistress of seduction with her drop-dead gorgeous looks. Looking for the queen of St. Louis' West End? Libra holds the title and the attitude to go along with it.

The novel is soaked with brazen sex and hardcore violence. You'll understand why when you meet Libra's girlfriends.

Books can be purchased at most on-line stores such as Amazon and Barnes and Noble. Books are distributed by Ingram. Contact the author at MaryLWilson2003@yahoo.com Or visit her at www.myspace.com/msghettoluv